Kayla's Redemption

Kayla's Redemption

Journey Series Book 1

Wanda B. Campbell

MICAH 6:8
BOOKS

Library of Congress Control Number: 2021919057

ISBN 10: 1-956607-00-5
ISBN 13: 978-1-956607-00-0

Cover Design: Tywebbin Creations
Cover Art: Leilani Jimenez

Printed in the United States

Kayla's Redemption
Wanda B. Campbell

Dedication

*This book is dedicated to everyone courageous
enough to start the Journey.*

Acknowledgments

First and always, I thank my Heavenly Father for entrusting me with the ministry of writing. My endeavor is to always make Him proud.

Craig, my husband of thirty-two years: Words cannot express how precious you are to me.

I'm excited about the next leg of our journey.

A special thanks to my forever readers for your patience as I balance writing and school.

As you read this first installment of the *Journey Series,* I pray you will be ministered to, as well as entertained.

The pandemic, climate change, and the quest for power has altered the world as we know it, but God's word never changes. He always takes care of His children.

Stay blessed and rest in Him!
Wanda B. Campbell

I love hearing form readers at:
wbcampbell@prodigy.net

Or, join the Facebook Group:
Wanda B. Campbell Readers & Supporters

Chapter 1

Kayla moaned as her head shook violently from side to side as she fought with her attacker. The thick and cold darkness shielded the predator's identity, but did nothing to conceal the marijuana scent that resembled a skunk. She used the odor as a guide to direct her fervent punches in an effort to stop the attack. Nearly breathless, Kayla's arms frantically waved in the darkness in search of an object, something to inflict pain on the individual viciously assaulting her body. Her achy bloodied fingers gripped something, what she didn't know. It was too dark to visualize anything. Whatever the metal was, it would serve as a weapon. Feeling a rush of adrenaline, Kayla slammed the unknown object in the direction of the funky marijuana odor. The voice, husky only minutes earlier, was reduced to a whimper. Her assailant pushed off her, spewing obscenities. Kayla didn't waste any time. She instantly jumped to her feet and ran without any sense of direction, screaming for help.

With every swift step she gained strength and momentum. In a matter of seconds, her muscular legs, courtesy of a daily exercise routine, and size-seven feet, carried her through the darkness and into a bright white-walled room. Kayla abruptly stopped and surveyed her surroundings. She was safe now. Certainly, her pursuer wouldn't launch an attack with all of these witnesses. The room was filled with both men and women scurrying about on a mission, to where, she didn't know.

A sea of green fabric blended with the white walls as dizziness began to overtake her. Loud voices from within the small room collided with the persistent beeping above her head, making the multiple conversations impossible for her to comprehend. The intense stares frightened her, causing her to blink rapidly. "Ms. Perez," she heard someone yell, just before surrendering to the dizziness and darkness.

Kayla attempted to turn her body so that she could rest on her right side. Like the countless times before, the sharp pain radiating through her right arm, prevented her from completing the simple routine task. She moaned and gingerly resumed lying on her back. It wasn't her favorite sleeping position, but at the moment, it was the most comfortable. Slowly, she opened her eyes and winced. The pressure from the wound above her left eye and the glare from the overhead light were too intense. Immediately, she shut her eyes. Not long after, tears pooled and trickled down her swollen discolored cheeks.

Softly, Kayla cried as once again reality set in. Three nights ago, after locking the doors to the national retail store where she worked as store manager, she was attacked by an unknown assailant. Unlike in her dreams, Kayla didn't get away. She was beaten and sexually assaulted then left for dead. If not for the compassion of a non-English-speaking Asian immigrant, she would be dead.

The Chinese woman, out on her morning walk, found Kayla near a dumpster at Emery Bay, unconscious. She was badly beaten and her clothes were torn. Fortunately for Kayla, the woman went home and returned with relatives who phoned emergency services.

Kayla wasn't sure she should thank Mrs. Yee or not. The pain plaguing her body caused her to wonder if she'd be better off dead. Her right arm was broken. Her stomach, legs and back were sore and bruised from her attacker's fervent kicking. Her face, Kayla doubted she'd ever be able to view her reflection again. The doctors assured her no facial bones were broken, but she didn't trust their opinion. They had also convinced her Morphine would ease her pain, but failed to mention the hallucinations.

With the back of her free left hand, Kayla wiped her cheeks.

"Mija, don't cry." It was her older brother, Carlos. He had been at her bedside. For how long, she didn't know. When she first regained consciousness, it was his demeanor that confirmed the severity of her wounds. Kayla couldn't recall one time she'd seen Carlos, who was well over six-feet tall with the frame of a bodybuilder, cry. Two days ago, her big brother broke down when he

3

saw her battered body. It took two orderlies and a security officer to lift Carlos Perez from the linoleum floor.

"Mama will be here soon," he assured Kayla. "She and Travis are flying into Oakland tonight."

At the mention of her mother and new stepfather, Kayla made another attempt to open her eyes. This time Carlos was standing over her, wiping her cheeks with a tissue. Briefly she held his gaze. His eyes were still red and puffy, but his expression was optimistic. Kayla knew he portrayed strength for her sake. That was the one thing she could always depend on from her big brother.

Carlos Perez, Jr., just two years her senior, had taken on the role of protector for Kayla and her mother following the death of their father at the age of five. From that time, Carlos had been the one constant male in her life and the most annoying. In high school, he transformed into Kayla's personal testosterone repellent. During her freshman year, the upperclassmen avoided her like she was infected with an incurable disease, thanks to Carlos' threats. If Carlos spotted a freshman speaking with his sister, he'd interrupt the conversation by lifting the youngster over his shoulder and promptly placing him in the nearest trash can. To make sure his message got conveyed, Carlos periodically returned to the school after graduation to make sure everyone knew Kayla Perez was off-limits.

"Did you tell Mama everything?"

"She knows you were attacked." He hesitated, before turning away. "I didn't tell her about the rape." He paused. "I couldn't."

Although he couldn't see her, Kayla nodded her head in understanding. She didn't know if she could break the news to Rozelle either. Just seven days earlier, her mother had finally opened her heart to love again and married a man who had been pursuing her for years. What is the correct way to inform a mother that her only daughter lost her virginity to someone without a name or face? Rozelle would be devastated.

"Do I look better today?" she asked, in an attempt to redirect her thoughts.

Carlos turned to face her. After a brief moment, he answered her honestly.

"Mija, you have a long way to go, but yes, you do look better. The swelling has gone down."

"I wish I wasn't in so much pain." She stretched her left hand toward him. "Can you help me sit up?"

"I'm so sorry about this, mija," he said, standing to his feet. "I should have been there to drive you home."

"Carlos, you can't blame yourself. I didn't tell you I'd be covering for the nightshift manager."

"No, you didn't. I'll fuss at you about that later," he said before adjusting the hospital bed to an upright position. He was gentle, but Kayla still moaned when he adjusted her body to accommodate the new position. He waited for her to relax before continuing.

"The police stopped by while you were sleeping. They wanted to know if you recalled any more details, like a description. I told them you hadn't." Carlos paused once again and looked away.

"What is it?"

After turning to face his sister, Carlos held her left hand. "Mija, you were the third assault victim in that area in the past ninety days." He paused.

"What are you not telling me?" she pressed. Carlos sighed heavily. "The two other women were also sexually assaulted, but you are the only one to survive."

"I guess I'm the lucky one." She attempted to smirk, but winced from the pain. Before she could prevent them, more tears streaked her cheeks. Sobs soon followed. "Why? Why did this happen to me?"

Carlos rubbed her hand and arm in an effort to comfort her. "I don't know, mija. But if I ever get my hands on that—" A knock at the door distracted him.

"Excuse me, Ms. Perez?"

Carlos and Kayla directed their attention toward the door, but didn't immediately address the Caucasian visitor wearing a clergy collar.

"I'm Chaplin—"

"I don't care who you are or what your name is," Kayla interrupted. "Neither you nor your religion are welcomed here."

Chapter 2

S am slowly and purposefully browsed the grocery
aisles. Being the product of a single-parent home,
he learned the value of a dollar early in life. Long
before in-store savings cards existed, Sam's mother taught
him how to clip coupons and browse the Sunday paper
for the best deals. Shopping without a grocery list and a
meal plan was considered sinful in Stella Jerrod's home.
Buying single quantities was unheard of. Stepping over
a discarded penny was a capital offense. On the few
occasions Stella allowed him to spend a leisurely Saturday
afternoon with his friends, Sam found his mother's
penny-pinching embarrassing. While his friends paid for
movies and arcade games with dollar bills, Sam counted
coins from a Ziploc bag.

Since moving from the south side of Chicago to
the Bay Area, Sam appreciated his mother's frugality. It
had carried him through four years of college and three
years of seminary. With careful budgeting, the money

from his part-time job covered his monthly expenses. By mid-month, several dormitory residents, most from upper middle-class, two-parent homes, would knock on Sam's door for laundry detergent or toothpaste. Sam was always well-stocked. Room 205, his room, became known as Sam's Club. The same could be said of his apartment today. At the moment, Sam's closets contained enough toilet paper, toothpaste, and deodorant to last him a year.

Being blessed with the position of Administrative Pastor at the largest church in Oakland didn't alter his spending habits at all. Sam faithfully did three things at the beginning of each month: deposited ten percent of his salary into the church's offering pan, added ten percent of his earnings to his savings account, and mailed a check to his mother for her to use as she saw fit. That was his way of thanking her for the many sacrifices she'd made for him and his three siblings over the years. He lived on the remaining seventy percent, which was a sizable sum.

As for clothing, Sam adopted the philosophy of "shop only when needed." His wardrobe consisted of one coat, five casual outfits, four dress suits complete with dress shirts and ties, five pairs of dress slacks for work, three sets of pajamas, one pair of sandals, Nikes, and dress shoes. His color choices were also limited. Stella advised him to buy black, navy blue, or brown because those colors were easy to coordinate. Today he dressed in black jeans and a black button-down flannel shirt, perfect for the nippy October weather.

Carefully, his eyes scanned the shelf for the item he'd marked off in the store's weekly sale circular. If his favorite spaghetti sauce wasn't sold out, Sam could make enough pasta to last him a week. He smiled with satisfaction at seeing three jars were left. All he needed now was fresh produce and a carton of his favorite vanilla ice cream. Sam tucked his grocery list into his pocket then steered his shopping cart toward the produce section.

He collected enough lettuce, tomatoes, carrots and cucumbers to accompany the spaghetti. Sam decided to treat himself to a fresh baked loaf of garlic bread from the bakery before heading to the frozen food section. Turning down the aisle, Sam stopped dead in his tracks. Suddenly distracted, vanilla ice cream was no longer a priority. The petite curly haired woman in the arm cast browsing the selection of frozen breakfast food held his undivided attention.

Her light-caramel complexion complimented the brown highlights in her shoulder-length hair. The puffiness under her eyes slightly distorted the almond shape of her dark-brown eyes with lashes so long and thick, they curved. Her lips appeared swollen and too large for her face.

Sam wondered if maybe she suffered from an allergic reaction to something. She looked exhausted, leaning against her shopping cart. Along with fatigue, Sam also saw fear in her eyes. Between selecting items, the young woman intermittently looked over her shoulder as if checking to see if someone was behind her. It was during one of those over-the-shoulder glances that she missed her aim for the shopping cart. Boxes of cinnamon French toast fell to the floor.

Sam, still captivated by her, hesitated before marching down the aisle to offer his assistance. The woman, who obviously had some anxiety issues in addition to the physical wounds, was beautiful. Being a minister didn't afford Sam the opportunity to casually date. His experiences with women were limited to an old high school girlfriend and a disastrous relationship with a fellow seminary student. Unlike preaching a sermon, he didn't have a technique for approaching women he found attractive.

Sam observed the woman struggling to gather the boxes with her free arm. She winced and before he realized it, Sam started down the aisle. But before he could come to her rescue, a tall muscular gentleman appeared by her side. Sam stopped and watched the interaction between the two. After collecting the boxes, the man rested his arm around the woman's shoulders. She leaned her head against his body. Sam lowered his head in shame. He had been captivated by another man's wife. Swiftly, he turned and headed for the checkout stand without the vanilla ice cream.

Outside in the parking lot, Sam watched with jealousy as the man lovingly assisted the woman into a SUV then closed the passenger door. To show her appreciation, she offered him a smile.

The affectionate display replayed in Sam's mind on the drive home. Observing that type of closeness reminded Sam of how much he desired companionship. At age twenty-seven, his life had been fulfilling. He had earned a degree in Business Administration and a Masters of Divinity. In addition to his position at church, Sam also volunteered part-time as a guidance counselor for at-risk youth. On a daily basis, he ministered to individuals about establishing a solid relationship with God. Sam had the spiritual part covered. What he desired was a relationship that would lead to marriage. Sure, there were numerous candidates at church, but not one of them held his interest as the fearful woman in the frozen food section had. Sam wondered what her name was and where she lived. Once again, he repented for coveting what did not and could not belong to him.

Minutes later, Sam pulled into his reserved parking stall in the underground parking garage at the apartment building he'd moved into ten days prior. After living a year in a studio apartment, the spacious two-bedroom unit within walking distance of the San Leandro Marina was a welcomed change. The view of the bay was spectacular and the drive from the complex to the church was less than ten minutes. He gathered his bags from the trunk. Instead of waiting for the elevator, he climbed the stairs to the second level.

As he approached his door, Sam shook his head in disbelief. For the third time in ten days, a package delivery service had left a package for his neighbor across the hall at his door. Sam sighed and unlocked the door to his unit. His success rate with connecting with his neighbor wasn't any better than the delivery company's. He'd knocked on apartment 212 three times, without an answer. Kayla Perez must be a very busy woman, he figured, with an addiction to online shopping.

Delaying what he assumed would be another fruit-less trip across the hall, Sam carried the box inside and placed it on top of the two other packages. He then put away his groceries and cooked the spaghetti. He enjoyed a satisfying meal and prepared lunch for the next day before finally making the trip across the hall to apartment 212.

With packages in both arms, Sam prepared to ring the doorbell. Before doing so, Sam practiced the few lines he remembered from his high school and college Spanish classes.

"Hola, Señorita Perez. Mi nombre es Samuel Jerrod," he stammered, when to his surprise, the door opened. He was even more surprised when the door opened completely, revealing an African-American woman with salt-and-pepper hair. Sam assumed she was Cuban and continued his bilingual effort.

"Yo vivo en el apartamento dos-cero-nueve. El—"

"Do I look like I speak Spanish?" the woman interrupted. She placed her hand on her waist and tilted her head to the side.

The gesture reminded Sam of his mother. Sam was taken aback by her forwardness, but relieved she understood English because he was running out of words.

"I am sorry. I assumed you were Spanish-speaking because of your last name, Ms. Perez. I'm new to the building and just wanted to drop off these packages the delivery service keeps leaving at my door."

"Come in," she said, stepping to the side to allow room for him to pass. "Set them over there on the table."

Sam did as he was told then quickly retraced his steps to the front door.

"Just so you know, I'm not Kayla Perez. My name is Rozelle Turner. Kayla is my daughter. She lives here, not me. I'm here assisting her until…" Rozelle's voice trailed off. "I am just here helping out for a while. When you meet her, speak English. Kayla understands less Spanish than I do."

He turned in the doorway. "Thanks for the heads-up. Hopefully, the delivery service will get it right from now on."

"Don't count on it."

"Mama, who is this?"

Sam turned in the direction of the hallway to see who the frantic voice belonged to. When their eyes met, Sam's breath caught in his chest. His palms instantly began to sweat. It was the woman he'd admired at the grocery store. Up close, it was easy to distinguish her mixed heritage. Sam also noticed the old bruise above her eye and wondered if she was in an abusive relationship. That would explain the cast.

He continued staring at her, not knowing what to say. He didn't trust himself to speak. Repenting twice hadn't erased his attraction to this woman, a woman he didn't know anything about aside from her name.

"Who are you and what are you doing in my apartment?" Kayla yelled her questions at Sam at the same time Carlos stepped in the doorway, arms loaded with groceries.

Sam still didn't respond.

"What's going on, mija?" Carlos demanded, dropping the bags to the floor.

"Calm down, Carlos." Noticing her son's balled-up fists, Rozelle offered the explanation since Sam appeared to be mesmerized by Kayla. "He's Kayla's neighbor from across the hall. He just came over to drop off Kayla's latest online shopping spree."

Carlos took more steps into the apartment and stood between his sister and the stranger. "If you're her neighbor, why doesn't she know you?" Carlos stepped even closer to him.

Sam remained tongue-tied, but inwardly began praying for protection. Sam was six-feet tall, but the woman's husband towered over him by at least three inches and he was broader. Sam was convinced now more than ever that the man was responsible for Kayla's physical condition.

"Carlos, leave that man alone." Rozelle pulled at her son's arm. "He's new to the building." She then turned to Sam. "What did you say your name was again?"

"It doesn't matter what his name is, I don't want him near my sister."

Sam blinked and breathed a huge sigh of relief. The bodybuilder wasn't Kayla's husband. He was her brother and from his overprotective behavior, Sam rationalized Kayla wasn't married. This Carlos would have chased off anyone attempting to get close to her. Sam smiled and extended his hand to Carlos. "I'm Samuel Jerrod. I recently moved across the hall in two-o-nine." Carlos ignored his hand. Sam then stepped to the side and addressed Kayla.

"You must be Kayla Perez, online-shopper extraordinaire."

Kayla raised an eyebrow. "Mr. Jerrod, you don't know me well enough to make fun of my slight shopping problem."

"A few more delivery trips and I will. Which is something I don't necessarily see as a problem," he added with a smile. Kayla slightly blushed then accepted his handshake.

Sam held eye contact with Kayla while shaking her hand slowly, mainly not to cause her any more discomfort, but also to savor the moment. Kayla Perez was definitely someone he wanted to get to know and not just on a friendly neighbor basis. Without meaning to, Sam squeezed her hand. Electricity raced up his arm after she squeezed back, causing him to suddenly disengage.

Kayla hung her head in embarrassment.

"That's enough, mister whatever your name is. You've served your purpose, now leave!" Carlos pointed toward the doorway.

"Carlos Esteban Perez, I know I raised you better than that." With one hand on her hip and a finger pointed in her son's face, Rozelle scolded her son. "This is not your apartment. And if it was that wouldn't give you the right to be rude. Mr. Jerrod hasn't done anything to you."

Carlos folded his arms and pouted.

"Please, Ms. Rozelle, Sam is fine." Sam voiced the words to Rozelle, but his eyes remained focused on Kayla.

"Well, Sam, please excuse my son. He's just a tad bit half-past crazy when it comes to his baby sister. Always has been." Rozelle continued talking about her son's obsessive behavior, but Sam wasn't listening. In his mind, Sam was calculating how he could prolong his visit. Rozelle noticed his silence and ceased talking. She folded her arms and observed the interaction between Sam and her daughter.

"Kayla, I see you're impaired at the moment. If you need anything, I'm across the hall. I'm usually home in the evenings."

Kayla smiled and nodded. "Thank you."

"She doesn't need your help," Carlos barked. Rozelle elbowed him in the stomach.

"Maybe I should leave you my number, just in case you can't make it across the hall. Or if you just want to talk."

"That would be fine," Kayla answered, much to Carlos' dislike.

"Let me get you a pen and paper," Rozelle offered.

Ignoring the grunts coming from Carlos, Sam quickly scribbled his home number on the paper Rozelle had handed him. He stepped closer to Kayla to give her the paper. She took a step back, but extended her free arm to receive the number. Sam flinched, not sure of how to interpret her action.

"Thank you, Sam," she said in a way that alerted him that was the benediction.

"It was a pleasure meeting you, Kayla and Ms. Rozelle." Sam then turned to Carlos, who was still brooding. "See you around." With that, Sam stepped over the grocery bags and into the hallway.

Chapter 3

L ooking into the mirror, Kayla traced every inch of her face with her fingertips. Her even skin tone had returned and the swelling was completely gone. Kayla had never considered herself beautiful, just average. Today, more than ever, she appreciated the small nose she inherited from her Hispanic father and the full set of lips from her African-American mother. Compared to what she looked like a few weeks ago, Kayla was now indeed beautiful.

Kayla raised both arms over her head and stretched. Mobility and range of motion were slowly returning to her right arm. Last week, she'd sent her mother home to enjoy her new husband. Six weeks had passed since the attack, and except for an occasional lower back ache, her body was back to normal. The emotional scars remained.

The police still didn't have a clue as to the identity of her attacker. That only added to Kayla's anxiety and fear of leaving her apartment alone. Whether the police located the perpetrator or not, Kayla had to overcome her fears and re-enter the world soon. She'd used up all of her vacation and sick time at the retail store. She was now living off of state disability payments and her savings. With limited income, her online shopping sprees were out of the question. Her doctor granted her two more weeks of disability and then it was back to work as if nothing had happened. As if a rapist wasn't roaming the streets. How was she supposed to pretend she wasn't afraid of a repeat attack?

Both the police and her doctor encouraged Kayla to seek counseling from a therapist or spiritual advisor. That was out of the question. Kayla was too ashamed to confide in a stranger and she resented God to the point where she wouldn't step foot inside of a church or hold a conversation with anyone proclaiming the goodness of God. She wasn't an atheist; she just didn't believe having faith in God was necessary. She didn't trust a God who allows horrible things to happen to good people for no apparent reason. He certainly didn't deserve her devotion.

Kayla began pacing around her apartment, trying to summon the courage to go jogging at the marina. A mundane task she'd performed every morning for the past two years up until the attack. She'd gotten dressed in fleece sweats for warmth in the cold November wind. Her pockets were filled with both a stun gun and mace, a whistle, and her cell phone, but she couldn't bring herself to leave the confines of her apartment. For three days, Kayla made it to the front door, but couldn't turn the knob. Fear and anxiety overtook her. She couldn't even make her weekly trip to the grocery store without Carlos. His work schedule prevented him from being available on Saturday mornings to jog the marina with her.

She considered calling her neighbor, Sam, to see if he would go jogging with her. Over the past few weeks, she'd done just that, beckoned his services because she was too afraid to leave the apartment. The first call, she asked if he wouldn't mind picking up a few items for her from the grocery store. He was very accommodating and delivered the laundry detergent and toilet paper in a matter of minutes. The second call was to borrow a cup of sugar. On each occasion, Sam was respectful and friendly, but she still refused to allow him inside of her apartment and wouldn't hold a conversation with him longer than thirty seconds.

She reasoned Sam was a good person, but fear prevented her from trusting him. Besides, she really didn't know him, not his character. What she did know was, Sam was a simple dresser with no social life. What else could explain why he answered her calls on the first ring? He was a strong, yet gentle man. She'd gathered that from his prolonged handshake. Unlike other guys, Sam wouldn't allow Carlos to scare him off. He smiled a lot and had a hard time forming words, at least around her. But he was handsome.

Weeks had passed and Kayla was still scolding herself for being smitten with Sam at their first meeting. She couldn't help it. Samuel Jerrod had the kindest smile with the cutest dimples and milk-chocolate skin. If Kayla wasn't closed to the idea of a relationship, Sam would be a good candidate.

"Maybe I should just call him." She voiced the thought audibly, but then quickly decided against it. It was one thing to send him on errands, but to use him as a babysitter was something totally different. Neither Sam nor Carlos could follow her to work in a couple of weeks. She had to make this first step on her own.

Kayla paced her apartment a few more times, filled her water bottle, added a pocket knife to her pockets and then slowly walked to the door again. An hour later Kayla was performing warm-up stretches on the track of the San Leandro Marina.

The November sky had traded in its brilliant blue color for gray clouds that hid the sun. The great Pacific Ocean didn't appear so magnificent now that the once rich blue rolling waves were a murky gray color. The overcast robbed her visibility of the Oakland and San Francisco skylines. The long San Mateo Bridge was still in view along with the Oakland International Airport runways. That was Kayla's favorite. Counting the number of airplanes landing and taking off made the four-mile run enjoyable. At the beginning of each run, she'd guess at the number of landings that would take place during her run, and then set her pace to beat it. Today, Kayla just wanted to make it around the mile track once before fear overtook her.

Due to the winter weather, the marina wasn't crowded with people. Kayla thought that was both a good and a bad thing. Less people on the trail meant the less people she'd have to watch. But what if something happened and no one heard her screams? What if the stun gun, mace and knife were not enough to scare an attacker away? What if she lost her cell phone and couldn't call for help?

Kayla closed her eyes and tried to push the frantic thoughts from her mind. "You can do this." She gave herself a pep talk.

"You have to do this. You have to get your life back." A walker passed her with a bewildered look. It was then Kayla realized she'd been speaking the words out loud. Now she was both embarrassed and afraid.

~~~

Rounding his second mile, Sam took a swig from his water bottle. The cold weather was perfect for jogging and so was the scenery. Overcast or not, Sam thought the Bay Area was one of the most picturesque places on earth. On a clear day the bay was postcard-perfect. Chicago had its skyline and Lake Michigan, but the Bay Area had it all. The Golden Gate and Bay Bridges, both Oakland and San Francisco skylines, Alcatraz and Angel Islands, plus the Pacific Ocean, not to mention the beautiful landscaping. Seminary led him to the Bay Area, but the diverse culture and moderate climate held him captive. Sam wouldn't feel cheated if he never experienced another Chicago winter again.

The one thing he did miss about his hometown was the people. His neighbors on the south side were friendlier than Bay Area residents. Where he was from, people greeted one another walking down the streets. Not so here. He figured people were too preoccupied with work, children and the high cost of gasoline to be cordial. Sam still made a point to speak and show himself friendly. So far it had paid off. He'd met a lot of interesting people and established some good friendships. However, at church his sociability backfired. Several young ladies mistook his cordiality as an indication of interest in a relationship. It took a meeting with the senior pastor to clear up the misunderstanding.

Nearing the half-mile mark, Sam wondered what he could do to initiate a relationship with Kayla or at least a conversation that didn't involve him running an errand. He'd been friendly and neighborly, but she wouldn't budge. The only time she had words for him was when she needed something. Then she would dismiss him. The other night, he'd gotten out of his bed to fetch her some sugar. To show he'd been thinking about her, Sam added the box of cinnamon French toast he'd picked up on his last shopping trip. She said thank you and then closed the door in his face.

Maybe she wasn't interested in him beyond a gofer, but there was something special about her. What? He really didn't know. She wouldn't give him a chance to find out. Maybe she'd experienced a bad breakup? It could be that her previous relationship had resulted in the bruises and arm cast and left distrust for men. Whatever the case, Sam was beginning to think he was wasting his time.

~~~

Kayla looked over her shoulder and let out a long sigh. She'd made it to the half-mile mark without an incident. Her legs were tight, causing her to run slower than her normal pace, but she was happy. Finally, she had won a round over the fear her abuser embedded in her psyche. She continued to inhale and exhale at a steady rhythm while silently encouraging herself to continue up the slope. Then she heard it. Footsteps were closing in on her from behind.

Kayla looked over her shoulder once again. The man dressed in all black wasn't there seconds before. She assumed it was a man, by the height. Kayla told herself not to panic at the same time she pulled the stun gun from her oversized pocket. The sudden rush of adrenaline carried her legs faster, but the footsteps drew louder and harder. A quick check over her shoulder again confirmed it was a man all right and he was gaining ground.

Beads of sweat framed her face as she approached another incline. She panicked. The nearest runner was at least a third of a mile up the pathway, too far to come to her rescue.

The footsteps were getting closer. So close she could feel the hair on the back of her neck standing at attention. She ran faster, but it was no use. A firm hand gripped her shoulder.

"Hey, Kay—"

"No," she screamed, turning around with the stun gun aimed at her attacker. Unfortunately for Kayla, the stun gun was aimed in the wrong direction with the charge facing her. She dropped the gun and ran in the opposite direction.

"Kayla, wait."

"Stay away from me," Kayla screamed and ran, waving her arms like a mad woman.

He ran after her. "Kayla, what's wrong?"

"Get away from me." She threw the pocket knife at him.

Sam had to think fast. Kayla was running toward the water to get away from him. He stopped running. "Kayla, it's me, Sam." He was too late. Kayla's attempt to station herself failed. She lost her footing and fell into the estuary.

Sam ran to the edge to help her out of the water, but didn't see Kayla. His chest muscles constricted. "Kayla," he screamed twice.

Her head bobbed and her arms slapped the water. "Help! I can't…"

Before Kayla could get the next word out, Sam was in the water and swimming toward her. With swift precise strokes Sam reached her before her head went under for a second time. After easily lifting her in his arms, he slowly maneuvered her back to shore, careful to keep water from Kayla's face.

With Kayla's arms tightly gripping his neck, Sam walked across the grass to an iron bench. He gestured to set her down, but Kayla, panting and gasping, squeezed his neck even tighter. Sam took the hint and sat on the bench with her in his arms. Once seated, she laid her head against his chest and cried like a baby.

Sam discerned there was more behind her sobs than what had just happened. He immediately began to silently pray for her. He continued to hold her until her breathing returned to normal and her cries subsided.

Kayla loosened her grip, but didn't leave the security of his arms. Finally, Sam broke the silence.

"Kayla, let's go home," he whispered.

She didn't respond.

"Come on, you need to get out of those clothes."

Kayla held her head up and looked at him as if she hadn't realized they were fully dressed and soaking wet. She didn't verbally respond, but nodded yes. She didn't move either.

Sam stood with her still clinging to him and carried her across the trail and across the street to the apartment complex in silence. He set her down at her front door.

Kayla reluctantly let go then shamefully lowered her head.

"Are you okay?"

She nodded yes again and proceeded to remove her key from her fanny pack. Her hands shook uncontrollably.

Sam took the key and unlocked the door, but didn't open the door. Kayla had never invited him in and he wasn't going to take advantage of her vulnerable state.

Kayla opened the door and stepped inside, but not before grabbing his hand, indicating she wanted him to follow her inside. Sam obliged her, but left the front door open.

Kayla stood in the middle of the living room, looking around as if she didn't recognize her surroundings.

"Are you sure you're okay?" Sam inquired.

Kayla moved her lips to speak.

"Kayla, where have you been?" Carlos roared from the open doorway.

Both Sam and Kayla's heads jerked in his direction, but neither spoke.

"Answer me, Kayla. I have been calling you for over an hour. I left work early when I couldn't reach you."

"I'm fine, now," she answered, looking back at Sam.

Carlos didn't like the implication. "What are you doing here? And why are the two of you wet?" Carlos balled his fists and walked toward Sam.

Sam met him halfway. That took Carlos by surprise, he stopped mid-stride.

"Look, man," Sam held up his hands, "save the big brother dramatics for later. Give her a chance to change first. She'll explain everything when she's ready."

"Who do you think you are?"

"Someone who's concerned about your sister's well-being."

"Man, you don't know me like that. I'll—"

"Carlos, please. Sam didn't hurt me." Kayla's voice trailed off. "He saved my life."

"What are you talking about?" Carlos looked back and forth from Kayla to Sam, like he detested being left in the dark, especially when it came to his little sister. His dislike for Sam mounted by the second.

Ignoring Carlos, Kayla turned to Sam. Again, she moved her mouth to speak, and again no words would come.

"Carlos, I'm leaving, but not because you want me to. Kayla needs to change and so do I. Do me a favor and don't badger her until after she's had a chance to relax." Sam then turned to Kayla. "Call me later, just to let me know how you're doing. Please."

After she nodded yes, they stood staring at each other for a long moment before Sam left.

"I don't like him," Carlos announced after closing the door.

Kayla rolled her eyes at him. "You don't like any man who shows an interest in me."

"I'm your brother, I'm not supposed to."

"You have nothing to worry about. There's nothing between Sam and I." As she voiced those words, Kayla wondered if they were true.

"It had better not be. I don't like him."

"That's because he stood up to you." Kayla started for her bedroom. "Make yourself useful. I need a new cell phone."

~~~

Sam arose from his kneeling position and sat on his bed. Praying daily was something he was accustomed to, but the fervency in which he interceded for Kayla was new. Three hours had lapsed since the chaotic episode at the marina, and every moment Sam prayed. He didn't know much about Kayla Perez, but what he did know concerned him. Kayla was afraid, terrified even. Of what, he didn't know. And she was hurting very deeply. Her pain echoed in her gut-wrenching sobs on that bench. He didn't need a revelation to know Kayla had experienced something terrible.

He rubbed his hands together, trying to figure out a way to get her to open up to him. Today, they had connected with one another on an emotional level. She was in need of the comfort and protection he'd provided. Sam wasn't sure what that meant, if anything at all. It was very possible Kayla wouldn't call him again until she needed something from the store. In the meantime, he would continue to pray for her.

Sam reached for his Bible just as the phone on his nightstand sounded. The caller ID revealed Kayla's number.

"How are you?" He was too concerned for her to waste time on small talk. There was a pause before he heard an uncertain response.

"I'm fine." More silence. By now Kayla would have made her request known.

"Did you mean what you said?" Kayla asked almost in a whisper. "About...about caring about me."

Sam shifted the phone to the opposite ear. He'd forgotten all about that statement. "Yes, Kayla. I do care about your well-being."

"But you don't know me. And after what happened today, you must think I'm crazy."

"You're right. I don't know you very well. No. I don't think you're crazy. I think you're—" Prompted by the Spirit, Sam redirected the conversation. "Have you eaten dinner?"

"No."

"Have dinner with me, Kayla."

She didn't readily respond. Sam assumed she was preparing an excuse to turn him down.

"It wasn't a question, but an answer to your question. This is a way for me to get to know you better, then I can tell you why I care about your well-being. Just for the record, caring for someone doesn't mean we have to be romantically involved. We can be friends." Even as he said those words, Sam acknowledged that was not what he wanted.

Kayla sighed into the phone. "I don't feel like going out."

"I'll cook."

"Can you cook?" she asked. "I thought bachelors couldn't cook."

He chuckled before answering her. "Come over and find out. Dinner will be ready in thirty minutes. Make it forty-five minutes. That will give me time to discard the old pizza boxes and two-liter soda bottles."

Kayla laughed. "Now you've aroused my curiosity. Should I bring anything?"

"Just your appetite."

An uneasy silence followed.

"Thank you, Sam," Kayla finally said. "For today… for everything."

"You're welcome." Her gratitude flowed like warm liquid through him. "See you in forty-five."

"Okay."

Sam sat motionless, staring at the telephone receiver, amazed at what just transpired. In less than an hour, Kayla would be seated at his dinner table, having dinner with him. It wasn't a real date, but it was a start. At least he hoped it would be. He wanted to impress her, but also learn the source of her pain.

Sam walked into the living room and looked around. The apartment was simple, but clean. Hurriedly, he straightened the books on his three-piece bookcase that attached to form one massive wall unit. He then fluffed and rearranged the couch pillows, removing all traces that he'd slept there the night before. The entertainment center was next. With record speed he placed his extensive CD and DVD collection in neat rows. After spraying air freshener, he then cleaned the bathroom. In just under twenty minutes, Sam had the apartment ready for his first female visitor.

All at once the adrenaline wore off and reality set in. A female he was attracted to was coming over. They would be alone. Sam second-guessed his impromptu invite. Was it wise, with him being a single minister, to have a single female in the confines of his apartment? His previous limited dates, found him in a restaurant or movie theater. He glanced at his watch. He still had time to make reservations somewhere. He'd decided to do just that, but then remembered Kayla said she didn't want to go out. After the trauma of that afternoon, Sam wasn't going to push the issue. Instead, he decided to call his best friend, Tyrell, also a minister, for advice. The two were accountability partners. When charting new territory or when one was weighed down with an issue, they leaned on one another for support.

Tyrell listened and agreed. Sam shouldn't press Kayla to go out, but also warned Sam to be careful by holding all conversations in the kitchen or living room and to only talk about safe subjects. The two shared a brief word of prayer before disconnecting. After the reassurance, Sam continued preparing for the evening. He'd just finished setting the table when the doorbell chimed.

Sam dashed into the bathroom to check his appearance in the full-length mirror before answering the door. Satisfied with his usual black slacks and gray polo shirt, he raced to the front door. He let out a long breath, opened the door then sucked in his breath and held in his throat at the sight of her.

He had never seen her this way. She'd traded in her sweats for a festive burnt-orange broomstick skirt with a matching scoop-neck tunic. Colorful embroidery lined the neckline. Her thick curly hair hung loosely at her shoulders. Her feet were enclosed in what Sam guessed were four-inch heels. Except for the hint of color on her lips, her face was void of makeup. Kayla was simply beautiful and smelled heavenly.

"You did get the memo about us eating in tonight, didn't you?" he joked once he finally exhaled.

"I got dressed just in case your food isn't edible," she fired back.

"You hurt my feelings." Sam pouted. "But you look great."

"Thanks." Kayla blushed. "You're looking at my last online shopping spree. I thought it was fitting, since it ended up at your place by mistake before finding its way to me."

He stepped back and gestured to her. "Come in." With what he thought was reluctance, Kayla stepped inside. "It's not as fancy as your place, but it works for me."

Sam closed the door behind her then offered her a seat on the couch.

"No thanks, I'll stand." Kayla interlocked her fingers then lowered her head.

It was definitely reluctance Sam sensed. Kayla was afraid to be alone with him. Before the night was over, he planned to learn the root of her fear. "Make yourself comfortable. Dinner will be served shortly." Sam left her alone in the living room and went to check on dinner.

"Sam, you have a nice place, but you could use some color. Your color scheme is so bland with all this black and brown," Kayla said after a few quiet moments had passed.

"Oh, really?" Sam stood in the kitchen doorway, wiping his hands with a dish towel.

"Yes," she snickered. "Your living room resembles your wardrobe."

Sam folded his arms across his chest. "How dare you insult the man who is preparing your meal?"

"Sorry, but you need some help in the color coordination department."

"And you need some help in the spending and planning departments."

Kayla braced her hands on her hips. "What are you talking about, Mr. I'm Afraid Of Color?"

Sam pointed a finger in her direction. "You know exactly what I'm talking about Ms. I'm Afraid To Buy More Than One Roll Of Toilet Tissue At A Time."

Kayla's hands fell to her sides and she threw her head back in laughter. "Okay, you got me."

Sam leaned against the doorframe with his hands in his pockets and watched her laugh. Her laugh was unusual, almost like a snort. It sounded wonderful. He thought to tell her, but was afraid she'd clam up.

"Did I ever tell you how much I appreciate you for going to the store for me?" she asked, knowing she had.

"I have a confession to make," Sam said, walking toward her. "I didn't go to the store. What I gave you came from my supplies. I still have your money."

"Supplies?"

"Come, I'll show you."

Curious, Kayla followed Sam down the hall to the storage closet.

"Wow," she said after he showed her his rainy day supply. He then went on to explain how his mother had trained him to shop on sale and to buy in bulk whenever possible.

"My problem is solved," Kayla exclaimed. "I'll just come here to shop. I bet you have some of those plastics bags with 'Sam's' printed on the side." She laughed some more.

"Make fun of me all you want. Just remember I'm cooking your food." The kitchen timer sounded. "Be right back." Sam hurried off to the kitchen. Kayla joined him a few minutes later.

"You had better be joking…" her voice trailed off. She didn't expect the display before her. "I thought you were cooking dinner."

Sam waved his arms over the table. "This is dinner. I made what I know you like to eat, only better." Sam pointed to each dish. "We have turkey sausage and fresh fruit. I wasn't sure how you like your eggs, I hope scrambled is fine. And your favorite, homemade cinnamon French toast. For your drinking pleasure, cranberry juice. Call it breakfast for dinner."

Kayla's voice was just above a whisper. "How did you know what I like? I mean, aside from the French toast."

Sam stood up straight. "I have another confession to make. I saw you in the grocery store the day I met you. I didn't know who you were, but I admired you from a distance and I remembered what was in your cart. I watched you drop the boxes and assumed Carlos was your husband."

Kayla remained silently stationed with her arms wrapped around her body, avoiding eye contact.

"Please, Kayla, don't retreat now." Sam gently took her hand. "Let's eat before the food gets cold."

Kayla wiped her face with the back of her free hand. She pasted on a smile then sat down. She waited for Sam to take his seat before piling her plate.

"Hold on," Sam said as she reached for the French toast. He regained her hand and said grace. Sam's eyes were closed. He didn't notice that Kayla didn't close her eyes or lower her head. She didn't say "Amen" either.

Sam initiated the dinner conversation by asking how she'd gotten her last name.

"My dad was Hispanic. He died when Carlos and I were young. We were raised around my mother's side of the family," she explained. "Before you ask, no, I cannot read or write Spanish. I can barely say a few words."

He then inquired about her work. Her voice strengthened with pride as she told him about the major retail store she managed. For the first time she relaxed and held eye contact with him. Sam wanted a second round of French toast, but gave her his undivided attention instead.

"If this was my last meal, I'd die a happy woman," Kayla said, rubbing her stomach after a second helping. "I love your French toast. Next time dinner is on me."

Sam raised an eyebrow. He doubted Kayla meant to say that last part. "You can show me some appreciation by helping with the dishes." Sam arose and began clearing the table.

A comfortable silence rested between them as they worked. Sam was praying for a way to approach the subject of what happened earlier that afternoon.

With the last dish dried and put away, Sam invited her into the living room. They sat side by side on the couch. Sam was careful to leave a space between them. After turning to face her, he gently took her hand in his.

"Kayla, I have enjoyed your company tonight."

"Thank you." Surprisingly, she smiled and made eye contact.

"You're an interesting woman and a very special individual. I would love to have you as a friend, but first I need you to tell me what happened today."

Kayla attempted to snatch her hand back, but he gripped it tighter. "Kayla, please don't run," he said gently. "I need to know what's wrong so I'll know how to treat you."

She lowered her head and immediately the tears fell.

"Kayla, what is it? Why are you afraid?"

She remained silent.

With his thumb and forefinger Sam lifted her chin, forcing her to look at him. In her soaked eyes, he saw it all: fear, vulnerability, pain, embarrassment, confusion, and longing.

"Kayla, please, I can't help you if you don't tell me. What made you run toward the water when you know you can't swim? What made you break down today?"

Kayla's lower lip quivered, but she didn't make a sound.

Sam continued praying inwardly. "Kayla, you can trust me. I won't hurt you."

With those words she broke down. For the second time that day Kayla found comfort nestled against Sam's chest. He rocked her until she finished releasing her pent-up emotions. He left her only to bring her some tissue. She blew her nose and they sat in silence. He resumed holding her hand and waited for her to explain. Before breaking the silence, she squeezed his hand.

"Six weeks ago, after locking up the store I was sexually assaulted."

Sam winced.

"I don't have any idea who it was. Neither do the police." Kayla paused then inhaled deeply. "After he raped me, he beat me and left me to die."

Sam's chest heaved as his emotions pushed to be released. His heart instantly broke for her. "Kayla, I am so sorry."

"I have been afraid to leave my apartment. Today was my first time out alone since the attack."

"If I had known, I would have never approached you from behind like that."

She looked at him questioningly. "Sam, I go back to work in two weeks and I'm too scared to leave my apartment. I don't know what I'm going to do." She broke down again and found comfort against his chest.

Sam wanted to cry with her, but she needed his strength. The flesh side of him wanted to hunt down the predator and lay hands on him.

"Have you talked to anyone about this? A therapist maybe? What you experienced was very traumatic. You can't keep it balled up inside."

She shook her head against his chest. "No. You're the first person I've told besides Carlos and my mother. The police suggested I see someone, but I just can't. I'm too embarrassed."

"Sweetheart, you have nothing to be embarrassed about." The endearing term rolled effortlessly from his tongue. "You're not the one running around inflicting pain on innocent people."

Kayla didn't offer a rebuttal.

Sam stroked her hair before asking the question. "Kayla, will you accompany me to church on tomorrow?"

Her head darted up. "No. I don't do churches."

He was taken aback by her hostile response. "What do you have against church?"

Kayla pulled totally away from him. "It's not church I hate, it's the God they pray to that I don't like."

Sam's face twisted. "Kayla, what are you saying? What do you mean you don't like God?"

"Let's just say, I'm not on the everybody-loves-Jesus bandwagon."

Sam abruptly stood to his feet and faced her. "God is a very loving God."

She stood face-to-face with him. "Then why does he allow horrible things to happen to good people? Why did he take my father? And what about…oh, just forget it. Under no circumstances will I ever step foot inside of a church."

Sam stared at her, stunned. He never saw this coming. He knew she had issues, but this was extreme in his opinion. What could have possibly happened to make her so bitter? "I can't believe what I'm hearing."

Kayla rolled her eyes. "Don't tell me you believe all that religious crap. The God is love song and dance."

Sam swallowed hard before answering. "Kayla, the church is my life."

"What?"

"I'm a minister. I serve as Administrative Pastor at Grace Temple and someday I plan to pastor a church of my own."

For what seemed like an eternity, Kayla stared at him with her mouth gaped open. Then without warning, Kayla ran from the apartment.

"Kayla, wait."

Chapter 4

Kayla turned onto her stomach and pulled the pillow over her head. If she tried hard enough, she could drown out the constant ringing in her head. Unfortunately for her the ringing wasn't a result of a hangover. She could sleep that away. It was the telephone.

The only person who would call this early on a Sunday morning was her mother. Kayla attributed her mother's rise-with-the-chickens mentality to the early childhood years she'd spent in Arkansas. Countless times Rozelle shared stories of having to cook breakfast for eight, wash the dishes, braid her younger sisters' hair all before walking a half-mile to the bus stop. Kayla knew some of the details were embellished, considering her grandparents moved to California when Rozelle was eight years old and none of Kayla's aunts and uncles would vouch for Rozelle's version.

None of that mattered this morning. Kayla was both mentally and physically tired. The first question from Rozelle's mouth, right after she asked how Kayla was feeling, would be, "How was your evening with Sam?" She now regretted her decision to tell her mother about Sam's dinner invitation. She had to tell someone, just in case Sam turned out to be crazy. It was either her mother or Carlos. No doubt her possessive brother would have ended the evening before it got started. She wished he had.

The ringing persisted. Kayla threw the extra pillow on the floor and surrendered to the inevitable.

"Hey, Ma."

"How are you feeling this morning?"

"I'm sleepy." Kayla held the receiver close to her lips in hopes the muffled sound would send her mother the message that now wasn't a good time to talk. It didn't work.

"How was your evening?" Rozelle asked cheerfully.

Kayla stretched her body then sat up with her back against the pillow before responding. "Interesting," was her one-word answer.

"Humm…interesting as in 'That was fun' or 'I can't to wait to see him again'?" Rozelle probed.

"As in, I don't think I want to see him again."

Kayla heard her mother's lips smack. "Kayla Alicia Perez, that's enough code talk. Give me details and don't leave anything out."

Kayla chuckled. The least she could do to repay her mother for calling so early was to keep her in suspense.

"Sam began the evening by criticizing my shopping and spending habits."

"I'm sure he told the truth," Rozelle snuck in.

"He went on to serve my favorite breakfast for dinner. And it didn't come from the freezer section. I helped him with the dishes. We sat down on his couch and I told him about the attack. I cried. He held me. He announced he's a minister. It all went downhill from there." Kayla relayed the events as if the evening didn't rock her foundation. Truth is, in that short period of time, Sam's gentleness melted the steel bars around her heart. She'd emotionally opened herself up to a man. Something she had never done before. None of that mattered now.

"Sounds pretty good to me." Rozelle was giggling. Something she'd been doing a lot since marrying Travis.

"Mother, he's a minister at that big church on Broadway."

"Exactly how is that a bad thing?"

"Mother, just in case you haven't noticed, I'm not into the whole God thing. I'm not sure I believe in God."

Rozelle's tone turned serious. "Now just a minute. I know I didn't take y'all to church every Sunday, but I made sure you were there for the important days. I had you and Carlos on the front row every Christmas and Easter. I made sure you learned those speeches by heart. So don't tell me you don't believe in God. You know all about God."

Kayla remained silent, listening to Rozelle ramble about her supposed belief in God. Rozelle was correct. Kayla had learned about the loving God who sent his son to die for the sins of the world. What Rozelle didn't know was everything Kayla learned as a child dissipated with her teenaged friend, Candace. "Ma, can we please talk about this later? I'm tired," Kayla whined.

"Okay," Rozelle conceded.

"Thank you. Talk to you later."

Kayla was about to hang up the phone when her mother said, "I'm so happy you were finally able to trust someone other than me and your brother with what happened."

"Yeah. Bye."

Solemnly Kayla replaced the receiver. Rozelle reminded her of how open she'd been with Sam on yesterday. She more than trusted Sam with her life. Worst, she trusted him with her heart. She made the mistake of opening up once, but never again and under no circumstances would she ever trust his God.

~~~

Sam sat at his desk, reviewing the Auxiliary Report from Sunday's services. Grace Temple was on the verge of reaching mega-church status. The current membership was just over five thousand with four services on Sunday. Including a service in Spanish to accommodate the Bay Area's large Hispanic community. Sam loved the diversity of Grace Temple. He had hopes of emulating its success in the church he intended to found one day.

There was a knock on the door, just before Minister Higgins entered.

"Hey, Tee." It was his best friend and confidant, Tyrell. He served as Grace Temple's Youth Minister.

"How are you this fine Sunday?" Tyrell helped himself to a chair and a miniature Hershey's chocolate bar from the candy jar on Sam's desk.

"Blessed and highly favored as always." That was Sam's usual reply.

"Did you get my proposal for the Youth Snow Trip?"

"Yeah. I'll read it over and shoot you a response on Tuesday."

Tyrell leaned forward with elbows on Sam's desk. "Now that we've got the business of the church out of the way, tell me more about Ms. Kayla," Tyrell asked, placing emphasis on the name.

Sam leaned back in his ergonomic chair and laced his fingers together. He could say many wonderful things about Kayla Perez, but her spiritual state would overshadow anything positive.

"Let's see. Kayla is beautiful and intelligent."

"That's good, beauty and brains," Tyrell commented. "Continue."

"She's strong, yet sensitive. She has the cutest laugh, or shall I say snort. She loves cinnamon French toast and is obsessed with online shopping." Sam stopped talking.

"And?" Tyrell gestured for him to continue.

Sam sighed. "And she's not the woman for me."

"How do you know? You've just met her."

"True, but I know enough to know we're on two different paths. That doesn't mean that we can't be friends though," Sam clarified.

"All you've mentioned are positives. What's the negative?"

Sam lowered his head, searching for the best way to explain Kayla's position. But there wasn't any other way to explain than to just say it. "Kayla doesn't believe in God."

"What?"

"That's not exactly true. She believes there is a God. She just doesn't like him very much."

Tyrell sank back in his chair. "Wow, man, that's deep."

"Tell me about it. She's everything I want, but she won't step foot inside a church of any kind." A moment of silence passed between them as Sam pondered the reality of his words.

"Maybe God will use you to lead her to Christ?" Tyrell offered. "Maybe that's the reason she's in your life?"

"Could be, but that will require much wisdom and patience." Sam sighed heavily.

"Pray about it. If it is God's will for you to show her the way, He'll give you the wisdom."

"I have been praying for Kayla all night and most of the morning. I still don't have an answer as to what my role is concerning her."

"Keep praying, God always answers." There was a knock at the door. "In the meantime, be careful not to get your heart engaged."

"Yes," Sam said, looking past Tyrell's shoulder.

"Hello, Pastor Jerrod." It was Jasmine, the Children's Church Coordinator. "Sorry I'm late with my report, but some of the parents lingered longer than normal after service." She extended the report out to him.

Sam stood to receive the paperwork. "Thank you, Sister Jasmine. In the future, just email it to me. That will save you a trip."

"Pastor Jerrod, I don't mind the walk, really."

Tyrell leaned back in his seat and observed the exchange.

"Whatever works for you." Sam returned to his seat. "Sister Jasmine, you and your staff are doing a wonderful job. I haven't received any complaints from parents."

Jasmine blushed. "Thank you. I appreciate the encouragement."

Tyrell cleared his throat.

"Oh, I'm sorry, Minister Higgins, I didn't mean to overlook you."

"Don't worry about it." Tyrell snickered and then looked at Sam. "I'm sure your business with Pastor Jerrod has your mind cluttered."

Sam ignored his friend's insinuation. "Thank you, Sister Jasmine. If I have any questions, I'll send you an email."

"Have a blessed week, Pastor Jerrod." Jasmine quickly scurried from the office.

Sam was certain Tyrell's comment had embarrassed her. "Brother, I'm going to pray for you. Why did you do that?" Sam asked once the door closed.

"Don't act like you can't tell Sister Jasmine is running for the office of Mrs. Jerrod."

Sam sighed and placed the paper into a file folder. "Yeah, I know. She's smart, attractive and loves the Lord, but there's no chemistry."

"Maybe not for you, but that sister is about to spontaneously combust."

Sam minimized the attraction. "It's just infatuation."

Tyrell stood with his palms planted on Sam's desk. "Maybe you can't see it because someone else is holding your interest," he challenged.

Sam arose and reached for his suit jacket. "Kayla and I are just friends, if that."

"Stay prayerful. Don't allow your emotions to take you places God is not leading you," Tyrell advised before stepping into the hallway.

On the drive home Sam pondered his friend's advice. He knew all too well how one's emotions can lead one astray. His last relationship was proof of that. He'd met Camille in his New Testament Greek class during the second year at seminary. For reasons unknown to him, comprehension of the Greek language came easy. Camille, on the other hand, struggled horribly. Sam offered his assistance and soon the two became study partners. By second semester they were spending all of their free time together. After consenting to a relationship, Camille introduced Sam to her parents and he accompanied her to family gatherings. Friends, family and faculty labeled them the ideal couple.

The beginning of his last year, Sam acknowledged that while he was attracted to Camille and enjoyed her companionship, he was not in love with her. Sam could not envision spending the rest of his life with her. Sam told her so the day before Thanksgiving break. Camille was devastated. She, along with her family, was expecting a marriage proposal at any time. Camille had even begun looking at wedding dresses. Three years later, he could still envision Camille on her knees, begging him to marry her. "I'm sorry, but God is not leading me in that direction. I care about you, but I'm not in love with you," is what he told her. The gentleness of his tone did nothing to numb the pain in her heart. That was the last time Sam saw her, on her knees, weeping for him. When he returned from the holiday break, he learned Camille had dropped out of seminary. Sam made a vow: The next time he engaged a woman's heart it would be the woman God has chosen for him. As he pulled into his reserved parking stall, he renewed that vow.

After retrieving his briefcase from the back seat, Sam pressed the power door lock button and headed for the stairwell. The multi-level building housed four elevators, but Sam loved the exercise. It was while walking down the hallway he thought of Kayla. He stopped at her door and wondered what she was doing and how she was feeling. Was she still afraid to leave the building? His curiosity fueled him into knocking on her door.

"Kayla, it's me, Sam," he announced, figuring she'd be fearful about opening the door. No answer. He knocked again and pressed the doorbell, still no response. He was about to give up when the door opened with the chain still latched. Kayla didn't say one word, only peeked through the narrow opening.

"How are you?" he asked, realizing he'd have to initiate the conversation.

"I'm fine. Anything else?"

Sam leaned forward so that his head touched the doorframe. He smelled mint on her breath. "Kayla, please open the door so I can talk to you."

"About what?"

"Last night."

When she didn't respond Sam turned and walked away.

"I thought you wanted to talk," she called out as he was about to insert the key into his door.

Sam turned to find Kayla standing in the hallway, wearing blue jeans and an oversized sweatshirt. Her hair pulled back into a ponytail and her face void of makeup. Her fists were planted at her waist and she wasn't smiling. Underneath her tough demeanor, Sam discerned the hurt little girl inside of her.

"Do you want to talk or not?" She patted the floor with her left foot.

Feeling the need to protect her, Sam walked back to where she stood and after placing the briefcase on the floor, embraced her. After a moment, Kayla's stiff body relaxed in his arms and she embraced him back. Her hair tickled his nose and her petite hands felt like pebbles against his torso.

"Friend, can we start over?" he asked once he released her.

"Come inside, I'll think about it." She stomped away before he consented.

"Lord, give me patience," Sam mumbled under his breath as he watched her ponytail bounce away.

Kayla sat with her legs tucked underneath her on the ivory leather sofa with her arm resting on the side. Sam sat on the opposite end.

"You clean up nice," Kayla commented in reference to the black double-breasted suit he was wearing. "Although, with the black tie you look like a mortician."

"You hurt my feelings." Sam pouted.

"I guess it's all one in the same. God and death. Man of God and Grim Reaper." Kayla didn't laugh or smile. If she intended to hurt him, she'd succeeded.

Sam's face hardened. He inhaled and exhaled deeply before responding. "Kayla, you are entitled to your beliefs." His voice was firm and authoritative. "But that doesn't give you the right to insult me. I take my vocation seriously. I have a right to my religious beliefs without you making a mockery of the God I serve." Sam arose to his feet. While reaching for his briefcase he added, "After last night I was hoping you and I could at least be civil, if not friends. Now I don't think that's possible. Bye, Kayla." In three long strides Sam was back at the front door.

"It's like that? You're going to walk out just because I said something you don't like? Some friend you are."

Sam turned around, but still held the doorknob. Kayla was standing now with her arms folded across her chest, smiling. Temporarily, Sam tried to maintain his resolve, but her goofy smile was contagious. She began to laugh and soon after Sam heard laughter pour from deep within his being. No one had ever manipulated his emotions as smoothly as Kayla had. In a matter of minutes he'd felt it all: rejection, acceptance, anger and joy. One minute he wanted to leave her presence, the next minute he wanted to hug her.

"Are we going to keep standing here laughing like chipmunks? Can we discuss this like two rational adults?"

"I am learning that there is nothing rational about you." Sam chuckled after returning to the couch. "Let's make a deal."

"I'm listening." Kayla relaxed her arms and then sat down.

"I won't try to convert you, if you won't try to corrupt me."

Kayla tilted her head forward. "Is that all you got?"

Sam's jovial expression turned hard. "Seriously, we need to set some ground rules."

"I agree."

Sam pressed his palms together and bowed his head as if preparing to pray. After a brief pause, he made eye contact and chose his words carefully. "Kayla, my spiritual beliefs are very important to me. They are the core of who I am. Without God there is no me. My life has no meaning." He reached for her hand and she yielded. With their fingers laced together he continued. "I don't believe in luck or coincidence. God allows everything to happen for a reason. He allowed us to meet for a reason. As of yet, He has not revealed to me what that purpose is. I have been praying for a relationship that would lead to marriage."

Kayla's eyes bulged.

"I admit, when I delivered the packages, I thought you were a possibility. But now I know that's not the case. I can't be romantically involved with anyone who doesn't believe in the God I serve."

"Good. I'm not looking for a relationship with anyone of any faith," Kayla interjected. "I don't have time for the drama."

Sam wanted to dig deeper and discover how much of that declaration was true, but didn't. For now, he and Kayla were on the same page. "I enjoy your company and would like for us to build a friendship." As he voiced the words, Sam was hopeful she'd come to know the love of God through his lifestyle. "I respect your feelings toward church and God for what they are: your feelings. I only ask that you respect mine. I can be your friend without forcing religion on you."

Kayla smacked her lips. "I doubt that."

"Not everyone I know is a born-again Christian. The director of the Youth Center where I volunteer is a practicing Buddhist and we get along just fine. We respect our differences. We don't force our opinion, but accept the other as being different. Not wrong, just different."

Kayla nodded as if she were processing information.

"Can we be friends?" Sam squeezed her hand. "You've been through so much, you could use a friend."

She squeezed back. "And you could use some color in your life."

Once again Sam found himself laughing at a serious moment. Figuring this was the best Kayla would offer, he accepted the moment for what is was—a step in the right direction. "I'll tell you what. I'll bring you on my next shopping trip, if you'll allow me to show you how to avoid going to the grocery store four times a week."

The sound of Kayla's snort-style laugh transformed into a melodious tune once it reached his ears. Why is this beautiful woman in my life? Sam asked inwardly, still smiling and still holding her hand.

Kayla pulled her hand away and stood in front of him. "You have a deal, Mr. Jerrod. Lead the way to coupon-clipping and penny-pinching heaven." She then saluted him like he was an army sergeant and she, the new recruit.

Sam threw his hands up and arose from the sofa, shaking his head. "I don't know what I'm going to do with you."

Kayla's playfulness suddenly evaporated. Lowering her head and rubbing her hands together, she asked, "Will you start by taking me out?"

"I don't understand?"

She continued staring at the carpet. "I need to leave this apartment and prepare to return to work, but... but..." Kayla's voice broke, giving way to a fresh batch of tears.

Sam used his fingers to lift her chin. "You're correct. You don't need more drama in your life. You are a bonafide drama queen. You have enough drama for ten people."

"What are you talking about?" She sniffled.

"One minute, you're mad, then happy the next. You're laughing one second and in the next breath you're crying.

Kayla pouted. "I'm a little emotional, that's all. I've been through a lot."

"Yes, you have," he said, looking down into her wet face. "And I'm going to help you in any way I can."

She bit her lower lip. It was then Sam realized how close his mouth was to hers. He freed her chin and took a step back. "Give me time to change and grab a quick bite then we'll go out."

"Okay," she said, wiping her face. "Where are we going?"

Sam retrieved his briefcase once again and started for the door. He held the door open before answering her. "It's a surprise, but trust me, you'll be safe."

~~~

Kayla crept nervously along the railing inside the Oakland Ice Center. Located in the heart of downtown Oakland and being the only ice skating rink in Oakland, the Ice Center was usually crowded. Today was no exception. Maybe it was her anxiety, she couldn't be sure, but today the crowd appeared twice its normal size. Kayla reasoned the holiday season was what brought the throngs of people out. Living in the Bay Area didn't provide for a Winter Wonderland. Ice skating around a rink decorated with garland while Christmas carols played overhead was the next best thing to having snow. Kayla had been on the ice for fifteen minutes, holding onto the railing. Six weeks ago, she'd be attempting a twirl and a double-toe loop by now.

She'd fallen in love with skating, watching it on television as a child. Ten years prior when the facility opened, Saturday mornings found her at center rink with the facilities coach. That all seemed foreign now, like it never happened. Closing her eyes, Kayla tried to recapture the euphoria she'd experienced on the ice. She envisioned herself, alone on the ice, gliding from one end of the rink to the other. She spread her arms and freely flowed to the music. When she reached the center, she twirled and twirled until…

"We can't hang onto the rail forever," Sam announced in her ear.

She opened her eyes and looked over her shoulder at her friend, wondering why she'd suggested they leave the complex in the first place. When she made the suggestion, she didn't know where would be a good place to begin her transition back into society. A crowded ice skating rink would have been the last place on her list. Leave it to a man to grab the bull by the horns.

"You said that already." She smirked.

"And I'll keep saying it until you let go of the railing," Sam retorted.

Kayla rolled her eyes before facing the ice. She wasn't mad, but irritated. She couldn't figure out how Samuel Jerrod pulled her from her comfort zone so easily. Today was the first time she'd ever stopped any man from walking away from her. Sam was handsome, but not worth her chasing after. She hadn't meant to stop him from leaving her apartment, but for some reason the idea of him not being in her life frightened her. It didn't set well with her that she'd become emotionally dependent on him. She didn't particularly care for the drama queen comment either, but Sam was right. She was an emotional mess, thanks to a vicious predator. She felt Sam's hands gently, but firmly grip the sides of her waist and nudge her forward.

"Come on," he urged. "I'm right behind you. I won't leave you."

Kayla scanned the ice. People young and old moved in every direction. Some bore smiles, others apprehension in their skating ability. Elation and raw energy covered the faces of the very young. Kayla chuckled, observing a young boy slip on the ice and immediately bounce back up. Kayla released the railing and like a magnet clung to Sam's hands at her waist. She wanted to move, but fear paralyzed her. What if her attacker was out there watching her? She'd been the only one to survive the attacks. What if he had been waiting for her to come out so he could finish the job?

"I'm here. No one will hurt you," Sam whispered in her ear.

With amazement, Kayla turned to face him. How did he know what she was thinking? She didn't trust her voice to ask, so she said nothing and faced the ice again.

"I'll protect you," Sam urged further.

Kayla felt her right foot move then the left. Sam moved with her.

"Good. Keep going."

Kayla continued moving, not because she felt confident, but she had to keep Sam's warm breath from her ear. The tingly sensation was distracting. With each gliding step, she gained momentum and self-assurance. Sam allowed her to control the pace and the direction. By the second lap around the rink, Kayla no longer held unto him. Thirty minutes later, the two were crisscrossing the rink with Sam struggling to keep up with Kayla's moves.

"What happened to that smart mouth?" Kayla called over her shoulder.

Sam was too busy panting to respond. She stuck out her tongue at the same time his skates got crossed. He tumbled to the ice, landing on his bottom.

"Would you like to hold onto the railing next time?" she asked in a voice that mimicked a child. "Or maybe you would like the kiddie rink?"

Sam laughed along with her, but remained on the ice until his breathing returned to normal then slowly maneuvered upright.

"Where did you learn to skate like that? You're pretty good."

"Thank you." Kayla beamed then interlocked her arm with his. Slowly they glided over the ice while Kayla shared her love for skating with Sam.

"Why didn't you pursue it? You have natural talent and definitely the body frame for skating." When she didn't readily respond, he asked the question again.

"My best friend." She paused. "We had plans to, but things changed." With that Kayla released Sam and skated away, but not before looking over her shoulder, making sure he followed. With fervor, Kayla moved across the ice, performing loops and turns. With the grace of a ballerina, she finished the impromptu routine with a perfect attitude spin. She didn't notice she had an audience until she heard the applause. Embarrassed, Kayla nodded her thanks then looked around for Sam.

Faces belonging to bodies of different colors and shapes crowded around her, but none of the faces were familiar. She couldn't see Sam. Her chest muscles tightened as fear gripped her. "Calm down," she told herself. "Just walk off the ice." She attempted to glide, but all of a sudden, her legs felt like lead. What came easily only moments before was now impossible. The temperature of the rink was set below zero, but her palms were sweaty and beads of perspiration outlined her forehead. A passing skater bumped her, sending Kayla tumbling on the ice. She lay there crying in the fetal position with her arms shielding her head.

"Are you okay?" It was Sam kneeling down beside her.

At the sound of the familiar voice and the feel of his arms enveloping her, Kayla raised her head. "Why did you leave me?" she questioned, her voice just above a whisper.

"Sweetheart, I didn't leave you." He used his palm to wipe her cheeks.

"But I didn't see you."

"I told you I wouldn't leave you and I didn't. I was with you the whole time," he insisted.

Kayla propped herself up on her elbows. "I looked and looked, but—"

Sam placed a finger to her lips to quiet her. "Just because you couldn't see me doesn't mean I wasn't here. When I give you my word you have to trust me. It's the same with our heavenly father. Just because we can't see Him doesn't mean He's not present and watching over us. We have to trust in His care."

Kayla twisted her face at that analogy, but didn't comment.

"Let's get out of here," he said, standing to his feet and extending his hand to her. "I have a taste for vanilla ice cream."

She accepted his assistance and once on her feet, interlocked her arm in his. She remained quiet, walking off the ice and into the locker area. She'd remind him about the God talk later.

Chapter 5

Happily, Kayla hummed the words to the Christmas carol playing on the overhead sound system. She couldn't remember the dance steps she'd learned in her fifth-grade class, but she could have created her own version of the "Jingle Bell Rock" right there in the retail store, had it not been so crowded. Today was more than her first day back at work; it was also the day after Thanksgiving, the official start of the holiday shopping season. When she pulled into the parking garage at Emery Bay at 5:00 A.M. the garage was already full. Shoppers lined the retail strip, with lists in hand and hopes of taking advantage of the early bird specials. The 9:00 A.M. register reading revealed sales in the first three hours equaled the entire month's intake. Kayla couldn't have been more ecstatic. Slowly, her life had returned to a semblance of normal, thanks to her family and Sam. With patience, each assisted her in adjusting to life after the assault. Her stepfather, Travis, a retired Oakland Police Officer, taught her self-defense moves and how to properly use a stun gun. Carlos and her mother accompanied her on trips to familiar places until she was ready to go alone. Sam, he was flexible and willing to adapt to whatever role she needed at any particular moment. If she needed a sounding board, he'd lend his ear. Sam escorted her on both jogs and walks around the marina. On more than one occasion, he operated as her personal chef, preparing her favorite, French toast. During shopping trips, he was in charge of strategic planning and budgeting. She conceded his planning saved her time and money. True to his word, Sam didn't try to convert her, but did reference scripture quite often. He didn't verbalize it, but Kayla had a strong impression Sam had added her to his prayer list. There were moments when Kayla felt the desire to say her own prayer of thanks to God, but ignored the urging from deep within her. This morning, being a prime example.

After being away from the store for eight weeks at the peak of the fall season, Kayla expected the store to be low on inventory and in disarray. To her relief, the store was well- stocked, complete with holiday decorations and reports from the regional office showed sales were up ten percent over the previous year. Kayla's first thought was to thank God, but then she reasoned the store's success was the result of hardworking and dedicated employees, not divine intervention. Kayla checked her watch. The face on her Seiko displayed one o'clock in the afternoon; time for her to relieve the floor manager for lunch.

"You can take your break now," she announced to Ashley.

Ashley unloaded the cashmere sweaters she carried into Kayla's arms and then exhaled heavily. "Thank you so much. I'm starved and exhausted."

Kayla nodded her understanding and instructed Ashley to take a longer-than-normal lunch period.

"Thanks, Kayla." Ashley quickly patted Kayla on the shoulder. "I'm so glad you're back. I really missed you. I didn't have anyone to discuss my crazy love life with."

Kayla valued Ashley's dedication and excellent performance, but her personal life could stand some major improvement. She estimated that Ashley changed men as often as she changed mannequin displays.

"Thank you. I'm sure you'll fill me in later."

"Would you like for me to bring you something back from Chevys?" Ashley offered.

"No, thank you. I brought my lunch."

"That's a first," Ashley replied, before rushing off.

Kayla restocked the sweaters and then the wool slacks that were on sale for fifty-percent off. A customer on a mission to purchase the last olive-green leather skirt approached Kayla with a request for her to climb a ladder and pull the skirt off the display. Envisioning record sales, Kayla was more than happy to oblige.

In the process of retrieving the garment, Kayla heard a familiar voice mimicking an overhead paging system.

"Kayla Perez, please report to the bottom of the ladder."

She looked down from the fourth step. Sam stood there wearing a big smile. Kayla grinned broadly and then hurried down and into Sam's open arms.

"How is it going?" he asked after a quick embrace.

"I'm good. You?" Kayla folded her arms across her body with the leather skirt on her arm.

"Better, now that I have my very own personal shopping assistant."

"Excuse me; can I please have my skirt?" The customer butted in before Kayla responded back.

Kayla's caramel cheeks flushed red. She'd forgotten all about the customer once she'd heard Sam's voice. "I'm sorry." Kayla apologized and then verified that the skirt was the size the woman was in search of. Satisfied, the happy customer practically skipped away.

Kayla turned back to Sam. "What's that you were saying about a personal shopping assistant?"

"I need your help picking out a Christmas present for my younger sister."

She raised an eyebrow. "And you come here on the busiest shopping day of the year?"

"You know me; can't pass up a good sale," he responded. "And with your discount, I'll save even more."

Kayla poked out her lips, pretending to be hurt. "And to think all this time I thought you wanted me for my brains."

"Discount first, then brains," Sam clarified.

The two shared a laugh and in the process gained the attention of nearby shoppers. Neither gave the impression they cared.

"Have I ever told you how much I enjoy hearing you laugh?"

"You can tell me about that after we select something for your sister." Kayla went into work mode. "What size is she?"

The next forty-five minutes consisted of Sam following blindly behind Kayla as she selected and then deselected coordinating slacks, blouses, skirts, and sweaters. In the end, Sam purchased three complete outfits for his mother and sister, including accessories, saving up to seventy percent.

"I hope they like the outfits," Kayla said, standing with Sam near the electronic security store sensor. Both of Sam's hands were loaded with bags; however, that didn't prevent Kayla from holding on to his arm.

"You have excellent taste. They'll love it," Sam assured her.

He continued staring down at her. Kayla perceived he had something else to say. "What is it?"

Sam placed the shopping bags on the floor and then gathered both of her hands into his. "Kayla, I want to ask you something that might offend you."

"Then why ask?" was her short reply.

"Because I want to share a special evening with you." She raised an eyebrow. "It's not a date," he clarified. "I've invited nearly everyone I know and have placed flyers throughout the complex."

Relieved, Kayla nodded for him to continue.

"Will you accompany me to the annual Christmas play being held at my church on Christmas Eve?" She remained silent. "What I should ask is, will you allow myself and Danté to escort you to the play? You remember Danté, right?"

"Yes, I remember you mentioning him a time or two." Danté was the seven-year-old he mentored at the Youth Center.

"Will you join us?"

Before Kayla could answer, Ashley entered the store and stopped mid-stride at the sight of Kayla holding hands with a man.

"Well, hello," Ashley purred, walking over and standing next to Kayla. "What did I miss?"

Once again Kayla's cheeks flushed with embarrassment. She stumbled through the introductions. "This is my Floor Manager, Ashley—hum—Ashley Davis." She then faced Ashley. "This is Minister Samuel Jerrod from Grace Temple Church." Kayla restrained a snicker as Ashley's jovial expression turned sour. Ashley's father was a pastor and after literally growing up inside the four walls of a church, she'd steered away from anything and anyone associated with church.

Sam released his hand from Kayla and offered it to Ashley. "Nice meeting you. Happy Holidays."

Ashley shook his hand then quickly excused herself.

"That's a first," Sam said, turning back to Kayla. "You addressed me as a minister."

"That's what you are? Or have I managed to corrupt you already?" Kayla made light of the situation and at the same time wondered if subconsciously she'd used the title to mark her territory.

Sam rejoined their hands. "You haven't corrupted me and I'm not trying to convert you. However, I would be honored if you would join me on Christmas Eve. The play and maybe ice cream, that's all. No preaching or throwing oil on you."

Kayla squeezed his hands and smiled. "Since you put it that way, I'll come on one condition."

"That I treat you to an online shopping spree?" he teased.

"That's not what I had in mind, but I'll take it," she said, excitedly.

"I bet you will."

Captivated by the inflection of Sam's dimples, she questioned her motive behind the offer she was about to make, but then reasoned that she would make the offer to any friend. "Would you join me and my family for Christmas dinner?" As the words rolled from her tongue, Kayla realized Sam was the first man she'd invited home for family dinner.

"Deal." Sam accepted without reservation. "I'd love to spend the holiday with you and your mother and stepfather. They're wonderful people."

"Don't forget Carlos."

"Don't remind me," he grumbled. A customer leaving the store tripped the security sensor.

"Sam, I have to get back to work," Kayla said and then quickly went to the customer's aid.

Sam thanked her again and then left, smiling.

In between assisting customers and restocking clothing racks and shelves, Kayla spent the remainder of the day warding off questions from Ashley about the nature of her and Sam's relationship. Ashley refused to believe that they were nothing more than friends.

"Since when do you hold hands with a man at work? I have worked with you for two years, and not once have I seen you interact that personally with any man, other than your brother," Ashley persisted. Kayla started to respond, but didn't. Ashley's mind was made up. It wouldn't matter how many times Kayla denied it, in Ashley's mind, she and Sam were romantically involved.

"Just for the record," Ashley said while replenishing a rack of evening dresses, "I think you would make the perfect minister's wife. Trust me, I would know."

The mannequin Kayla was dressing hit the floor with a loud bang.

Chapter 6

S am opened his mirrored closet doors and weighed his options. For the first time in his life, he wished for a more complex wardrobe. The bland colors no longer sufficed. As he roamed the hangers loaded with the all-too-familiar clothing, Sam questioned if the dark and simple clothing had ever satisfied him. Or, had he simply adopted his mother's standards as his own? He didn't know. It wasn't that he couldn't afford more contemporary and colorful clothing, but his upbringing had trained him to be happy with less. Then there was Kayla. Hearing her poke fun at his taste in clothing sparked a desire for change. Was he trying to please her? He rationalized that was not the case, but he did value her opinion and held the highest respect for her. She still harbored issues with God and ironically enough, her indifference was what kept him drawn to her.

He'd kept his word. He didn't preach to her or pressure her. Instead, he focused on being a good friend to her, and like any good Christian friend would do, Sam prayed for her daily. The more he prayed, the more connected he felt to her. The effects of his fervent prayers were evident.

Kayla's anxieties were subsiding and so were her, what Sam labeled as, drama swings. She smiled more and allowed herself to relax, at least with him. She'd reached a level of comfortability to where she now popped up at his door with a plastic grocery bag in hand and helped herself to his supplies.

With this being the week leading up to Christmas, he hadn't seen much of her. They did, however, talk on the phone twice a day. He'd listen to her recap the highlights of holiday shoppers gone wild, and then she'd listen to him share details about his escapades with Danté. The conversations were good, but he missed her presence. Sam looked forward to spending the evening with two of his favorite people. The more he thought about Kayla and Danté, the more he realized how similar they were.

He'd met both after traumatic events and both were initially afraid to trust him. Danté Thomas and his mother were victims of his now-absent father's abuse. During their first meeting, Danté refused to talk. He sat in the same spot with his head bowed the entire hour. Now, three months later, Sam could barely get a word in. Like Kayla, Danté would be upset if Sam was late picking him up.

Sam grabbed his black dress slacks, a white dress shirt, and a black checkered tie and closed the closet doors. He quickly dressed and after checking himself in the mirror, decided a shopping trip was in order. He knocked on Kayla's door with seconds to spare.

Kayla opened the door and much to his surprise she didn't have her purse and coat in hand. Instead, she invited him inside and then instructed him to have a seat on the couch before disappearing into her bedroom.

Sam obeyed without reminding her of the time. Kayla was too beautiful for him to fuss. In that brief interaction, Sam examined her from head to toe. The red dress fit her perfectly and with her hair pinned up, she resembled a princess. The red matching heels added definition to her already-shapely legs.

"Here," she said holding out a long slender box with a decorative bow and ribbon attached. "It's your Christmas present. I would wait until tomorrow, but you really need this now."

The gesture left Sam nearly speechless. He wasn't expecting a Christmas gift from her, although he'd purchased one for her. He stood and humbly accepted the box from her.

"Thank you, Kayla. This is definitely a surprise."

Kayla's right hand immediately flew to her waist. She cocked her head to the side. "A surprise? Are you trying to say that I am too selfish to buy a present for a friend?"

"Save the drama for the play," Sam said and at the same time removed the ribbon.

Kayla rolled her eyes, but then smiled when his grin nearly reached his eyes.

"Sweetheart, thank you," he said, holding up the tie that matched her dress. "You're right, I do need this now." Sam set the box on the couch and began removing his black tie from around his neck.

"There's more; let me show you." Kayla picked up the box and after moving tissue paper around, held up four additional ties, all containing bright colors and contemporary designs.

Sam finished tying the new tie around his neck, and then admired the others. Sam was certain the soft material beneath his fingertips was silk.

"These are absolutely incredible. You shouldn't have."

Kayla moved closer and straightened his new tie. "Oh, yes, I should have. You need plenty of help, buddy."

"And you're perfect for me." Kayla raised an eyebrow.

"I mean, you're the perfect person to bring color into my life."

"Yeah, whatever," Kayla said, reaching for her coat. "It's time to go."

Sam exhaled slowly, relieved that she'd stepped away from him. Her perfume had nearly rendered him intoxicated. He quickly replaced his new tie collection inside the box and then assisted Kayla with her coat. The sooner fresh cold air hit his face, the sooner he'd remember that romantically, Kayla was off-limits.

The ride to Danté's apartment complex was quiet, except for the classical music playing on the satellite radio station. He glanced over at Kayla. She looked happy.

"Thank you for coming," he said, laying his hand on top of hers. "This means so much to me." That moment Sam identified the excitement that had been bubbling in the innermost part of his being since Kayla agreed to accompany him to the play. He was happy to finally share some form of his spiritual life with Kayla.

"Just remember, I'm not getting in any prayer lines." Kayla reminded him of his promise.

"No need," Sam said after pulling up to the curb. "I pray for you every day myself."

"I knew it," she exclaimed just as a little hand tapped the passenger window.

Sam got out and darted around to the passenger side. He and Danté exchanged high-fives. Before securing the child into the seatbelt, Sam waved bye to his mother.

"Oh, Sam, he's adorable," were the first words from Kayla's mouth when Sam re-entered the vehicle. "You didn't tell me how cute he is."

Sam faced the back seat. "Danté, this is my friend, Ms. Kayla, I told you about."

"Hello, Ms. Kayla." Danté smiled then looked over at Sam.

"She's pretty." Danté giggled.

"Thank you, cutie." Kayla rummaged through her purse. "I think I have some peppermint candy in here for you."

"Thank you." Danté giggled when she handed him the candy.

"Whatever you need, just let me know." Kayla twisted in her seat and talked to Danté the entire ride, excluding Sam from the conversation about school, television, and books.

The two were still chatting when Sam pulled into his reserved parking space inside the church's parking lot.

Captivated by the seven-year-old, Kayla didn't wait for Sam to open the door for her. By the time Sam had reached her door, she had opened the rear passenger door for Danté and was now holding his little hand.

Sam studied her for a moment. This was the first time he'd seen the maternal caring side of Kayla. His eyes traveled to Danté's beaming smile and bright eyes, and for a brief moment imagined what his offspring with Kayla would look like. Shaking his head from side to side, Sam rebuked the thought. However beautiful and caring, Kayla was not the woman God had for him. "Shall we?"

Sam and Kayla walked through the parking lot and inside the building with Danté between them.

~~~

Kayla's steady stride came to an abrupt halt once her feet touched the magenta carpet leading into the main sanctuary. Her grip on Sam's hand tightened as she stood there beholding the scenery. Grace Temple didn't bear any resemblance to the church she'd attended years ago on special occasions. The old square building, parking lot included, could easily fit four times inside the dome-shaped building with room to spare. The sanctuary had the appearance of a concert hall with its theatre-style seating and high-vaulted ceilings. Absent was the traditional pulpit. In its place, a raised platform lined with poinsettias and mounted speakers. Instead of stained-glass windows, magenta fabric outlined with gold trim lined the walls. High above the choir stand, which Kayla estimated to seat one hundred persons, hung a huge wooden cross with magenta fabric draped over it. Kayla removed her suddenly sweaty palm from Sam's hand and grabbed his arm with both hands. She had assumed the church had a large membership by its size, but the idea that the sanctuary would be full for a play, never crossed her mind. Except for the first two rows, nearly every seat in the one-thousand-seat sanctuary was full. Instantly, she regretted her decision to step foot inside of a church again.

"What's the matter?" Sam whispered in her ear.

"I-I," she stuttered. "I didn't know so many people would be here."

"You're safe. Can't anything bad happen to you while you're in God's house. Come on, let's take our seats." Sam started down the side aisle, holding Danté's hand with Kayla beside him.

Kayla wanted to inform him that not everyone was safe within the four walls of a church. That the place of peace and joy could also be a source of hell, but she didn't say anything, just simply followed.

"Do we have to sit so close?" Kayla protested before Sam turned down the first row. "Any closer and we'll be on the stage. Besides, these seats are marked reserved."

Sam stopped and spoke gently to her. "Kayla, you forget, I am the Administrative Pastor here. I am required to sit up front alongside the Senior Pastor and his family. I hope you're comfortable with that."

She wasn't comfortable with that, but before she could voice her opinion, the members in close proximity began greeting Sam.

"Merry Christmas, Pastor Jerrod."

"God bless you, sir."

With the meekness of a servant, Sam returned each greeting.

Tyrell approached from behind. "Sam? I mean, Pastor Jerrod, is that you?"

Sam twisted his face. "What kind of question is that?"

"You look different in color. I'm used to the black-and-white version." Tyrell chuckled. "Nice tie."

Kayla laughed also. "I told you, you needed help."

Tyrell looked over at Kayla then down at Danté. "You must be Danté," he said, squatting down to his level. "I hear you're a Raiders' fan?"

Danté giggled and nodded his head in affirmation. "I'll see if I can talk Sam into taking us to a game," he whispered to Danté.

"I heard that," Sam called from above.

Tyrell arose to his full height and then extended his hand to Kayla. "I'm sorry, but I haven't heard anything about you."

"Please excuse my bad manners," Sam interrupted. "This is my best friend, Tyrell Higgins. He's the Youth Minister here." He then turned to Tyrell. "This is my friend, Ms. Kayla Perez."

"Kayla?" Tyrell questioned with his hand extended.

She leaned closer to Sam before accepting Tyrell's handshake. "Hello," she said softly.

"I stand corrected. I have heard about you. Welcome to Grace Temple. I pray you have a pleasant experience."

"Thank you," she said, wondering just what Tyrell had heard.

"The play will be starting soon," Sam announced after checking his watch. "We should be seated."

"Pastor Jerrod."

All three adults turned to see who'd called Sam's name. It was Jasmine.

"Hello, Pastor Jerrod," she said nearly breathless and then acknowledged Tyrell with a nod. "I've been waiting for you."

Already Kayla didn't like this woman. She didn't even know her name yet, but Kayla didn't like the way Sam's name rolled off her tongue.

"Is there a problem, Jasmine?" Sam asked with concern.

"No problem. I was just wondering if you wanted some company tonight," she clarified.

Kayla moved so close to Sam, her hair grazed Sam's tie. If the coordinating dress and tie didn't do the trick, Kayla hoped the move would convey the message that Pastor Jerrod already had sufficient company.

Jasmine stared down into Kayla's face then back up at Sam's.

"Thank you for the offer," Sam began. "But I'm here with my friends, Kayla and Danté." He gestured toward Danté, whose head bobbed from one woman to the other.

"Oh, I see," Jasmine said slowly and then forced a smile. "Nice tie. The color looks good on you."

A full grin creased Sam's face. "Thank you. It's a Christmas gift from Kayla." Sam, oblivious to Jasmine's discomfort, continued talking excitedly. "If you think this is nice, wait until you see the other ones she picked out."

Jasmine was smiling, but Kayla could tell she was on the verge of crying. Her woman's intuition told her the woman in the hunter-green dress held a greater interest in Sam than he had in her.

Tyrell cleared his throat. Senior Pastor Simmons had entered through the side door and headed in their direction.

Sam greeted Pastor Simmons and his wife and then introduced Kayla and Danté.

Although respectful, Kayla's greeting lacked sincerity. If Pastor Simmons felt her disposition, he didn't show it. He shook her hand and welcomed her to Grace Temple then went on to greet Tyrell and Jasmine.

"Take your seats, the play's about to start," Pastor Simmons instructed.

Sam and Kayla walked down the row and sat down with Danté between them. Sam reached over and tapped Kayla on her leg. "Thank you again for coming," he said just before the lights dimmed.

"We need to talk," Tyrell whispered to Sam.

For reasons Kayla couldn't identify, she felt disappointed that the play performed wasn't the traditional story of Jesus' birth. She'd assumed with it being Christmas time that a baby doll masquerading as baby

Jesus would be wrapped in swaddling clothes. She would soon learn that very little about Grace Temple was traditional.

The play, titled *The Father's Love*, depicted God's close relationship with his son in heaven, the love God carried for the world and Him struggling with the decision to offer the ultimate sacrifice.

Kayla's eyes misted during the opening scene and remained wet throughout the entire drama. The scenes in which God nurtured the son resurrected the longing Kayla had for her deceased father's touch. Feelings Kayla considered dead and buried sprouted to the surface and manifested in a steady flow of tears.

"What's wrong with Ms. Kayla?" Danté whispered to Sam.

Sam, also captivated by the illustration, wasn't aware of Kayla's silent tears. At Danté's prompting, he glanced over at Kayla. Tears dripped from her chin. He pulled out his handkerchief from his inside pocket, then reached across Danté to hand it to her. Kayla took it without looking in his direction. In the final scene of the play, God tearfully sends his son away on a mission to redeem mankind. As the actor playing the son disappeared, a spotlight illuminated the wooden cross. The magenta fabric had been replaced with white sheets with red markings. The organist struck a chord and a tenor voice filled the sanctuary with the words to "The Old Rugged Cross."

With both hands covering her mouth to muzzle the sound, Kayla bent over and released sobs that shook her body. Deep within she ached for the love demonstrated on stage and at the same time grieved for not being found worthy of that love. The play portrayed a loving and giving God, but all he'd ever done was take from her. First, her father, then Candace and now her virtue. God seemed to love everyone, but her.

When the song ended, the melody continued to play softly. Pastor Simmons, along with the ministerial staff, Sam included, lined the stage. Slowly and methodically, Pastor Simmons extended the invitation to receive salvation to those who hadn't, but would like to experience the love of God, to come forward.

From the stage Sam prayed fervently for Kayla. He inhaled deeply when she stood to her feet and then sighed heavily as he watched her leave the sanctuary.

Sam and Danté found her waiting near the exit after the dismissal.

"Are you sick, Ms. Kayla?" Danté asked.

Kayla smiled before grabbing his hand. "No, sweetie, I'm all better now." She led Danté outside without addressing Sam.

Chapter 7

"Father, I thank you for allowing me to once again see the day set aside to celebrate Your unselfish love in sacrificing your only begotten Son. Thank you for loving me so much. Today and every day presents opportunities for me to express Your love to others. I ask this in Your Son Jesus' name. Amen."

At the close of the prayer Sam lifted from his kneeling position and sat on the side of his bed. The clock on his nightstand read 5:59 a.m., just one more minute before he would hear his mother's voice. Since his move to California they had an agreement to phone one another at 6:00 a.m., Pacific Standard Time, on Christmas morning. This morning overwhelming joy filled his heart for two reasons. One, he was grateful to be alive and in good health. Second, he believed God had softened Kayla's heart through the play. She didn't voice it last night; in fact, Kayla didn't say one word on the ride back to the complex after he dropped off Danté. She didn't even say good night when he walked her to her door. But Sam felt in his heart that she was on her way to establishing a personal relationship with Christ.

Did that renew his desire to have more than a platonic relationship with Kayla? No. His feelings for Kayla had not changed. She was off-limits.

He'd rehearsed those very words with Tyrell last night. The two had private words briefly after dismissal.

"How did you manage to convince Kayla to attend the play? More importantly, when did the two of you become an item?" Tyrell questioned.

"I convinced her to attend by promising not to pressure her. I think the message in the play spoke volumes," Sam explained. "We are not romantically involved, just two people enjoying each other's company."

"Is that all?"

"Nothing more," Sam insisted.

Tyrell nodded slowly before responding, as if he were pondering something. "Be careful, man. Your actions are not lining up with your words. Neither are Kayla's."

Sam twisted his face, expressing confusion. "What do you mean?"

"Man, you're glowing. And don't tell me you didn't notice the way Kayla marked her territory with Jasmine."

Sam had noticed, but justified her actions. "Kayla was just nervous."

Tyrell waited before responding. "Has God shown you what your role is in her life?"

Sam didn't have an answer, at least not one that made sense. He prayed more times than he could count for

Kayla and the only answer he received was to be patient and gentle with her. Until when and leading up to what, he didn't know.

"Kayla and I are meant to be friends. Beyond that and for how long, I don't know." Sam spoke the words looking over Tyrell's shoulder at Danté still seated.

Tyrell patted his left shoulder. "Just be careful. Connecting your heart to the wrong person is a devastating experience."

A picture of Camille flashed before Sam. "I know," he said solemnly.

The two exchanged holiday wishes and then parted. Reflecting back now, Sam wondered if there was more his friend wanted to say. If so, he'd hear about it soon enough. Tyrell had never been one to bite his tongue.

The telephone sounded at exactly 6:00 a.m. Sam cheerfully answered the phone. "Merry Christmas, Mama."

"Merry Christmas, baby." His mother's voice reminded Sam of the legendary Lena Horne. Stella Jerrod was regal and sophisticated in an economical kind of way and beautiful. "Did your gifts arrive in time?"

"The box arrived two days ago. Thanks, Mom." Every Christmas Sam could depend on two things: a phone call from his mother and a box filled with white T-shirts, Hanes underwear, socks, and flannel pajamas. Stella believed in practical gifts.

"Did you and Rachelle like your presents?"

"They're lovely, baby. Thank you." She paused and Sam waited patiently for her to continue. "And so many. I know you're doing well, but I wasn't expecting all this."

Sam knew his mother well; he remained quiet.

"Everything is all color-coordinated and the right size. I just love those earrings. It's about time."

"Huh?" The last statement caught Sam off guard.

"Since you're not going to tell me, I'll ask. Who is she?"

Laughter erupted from Sam and echoed though his bedroom.

"Don't act like you picked out all that fancy stuff by yourself. And didn't no ordinary sales clerk get you to spend this kind of money."

Sam composed himself long enough to answer. "My neighbor, Kayla, is the manager of a major retail store. Actually, she selected everything. I basically nodded and then handed her cash."

"I see," Stella said, then asked, "How well do you know this—what's her name again?"

"Kayla, Mom. Her name is Kayla Perez." Sam went on to share how they met, without revealing Kayla's physical and emotional condition. He mentioned ice skating, cinnamon French toast, and teaching her how to shop. Not once did he mention Kayla's stance with God. Stella Jerrod would not approve of any relationship of any kind with someone who doesn't believe in God.

"I see," Stella said again. "Are you this close to all of your neighbors?"

"I know what you're thinking; we're just friends, Mama."

"I see," Stella said for a third time, confirming for Sam she felt there was more to the story. "I look forward to meeting her someday." Stella asked him about his plans for the day. Once again, she was quiet after she heard of his plans to have dinner with Kayla and her family.

"Mama?"

"I'm here, baby," Stella answered after clearing her throat. "Let me put Rachelle on the phone, before we use up your minutes.

Sam heard her call his younger sister without reminding his mother he had unlimited minutes. "Samuel, I'll be praying for you and Kayla," Stella said before handing the phone to her daughter.

"So, you have a girlfriend?" were the first words from Rachelle's mouth. Once again Sam defined his relationship with Kayla all the while wondering if his definition was correct, considering he'd imagined having children with her.

~~~

Except for special occasions, Kayla limited her makeup to light lip color and occasional eye shadow, but this morning she needed help. A sleepless night of tears left her face in need of a complete makeover, foundation included. The glamorous face staring back at her concealed the bags underneath her eyes, but did nothing to calm the torrential winds that ravaged her emotions throughout the night.

Lying in bed with both the radio and television on was useless last night. Nothing was effective in erasing the image of the wooden cross draped with the white red-stained fabric. Kayla remembered every scene from the play vividly. Throughout the night, scenes randomly flashed before her along with Pastor Simmons' invitation to connect to the body of Christ. For a brief moment last night, Kayla considered accepting the invitation. Then thoughts of Candace rushed back, causing Kayla to once again reject the love Christ and the church offered.

So many questions bombarded her mind, but the one that stood out the most had her wondering if the entire congregation of Grace Temple was mentally challenged for believing in the whole God-is-love propaganda. The people were friendly and happy. Happy to the point Kayla doubted they experienced any pain at all. Life had obviously dealt them a hand with a free pass on sorrows. She suspected none of them had lost a friend at the hand of the church. Kayla would bet her paycheck none of the happy-go-lucky church women had their virginity stolen and forced to live in fear. God certainly had his picks and chooses when it came to extending his love.

"This is crazy," she mumbled at her reflection. "Here it is Christmas morning and I'm devaluing the whole premise behind the day." She stared a while longer and debated if the congregation of Grace Temple was sane and she, the crazy one. Before she reached a resolution, the doorbell sounded. As always, Sam was punctual. Good thing because she needed to set him straight about this conversion thing. He'd kept his promise not to pressure her, but he'd blindsided her with the play. He had to have known the effect the drama would have on her. Had she gained control of her emotions, she would have told him off last night. He'd get a double portion of drama now that she was irritated and fatigued from lack of sleep.

Kayla applied a coat of lip gloss before stomping to the door. She looked through the peephole and then swung the door open.

"Samuel Jer—" The words hung in her throat once her eyes caught sight of the decorative package with the big red bow.

"Merry Christmas, Kayla." Sam's grin nearly showed all thirty-two teeth.

Kayla's heavily exhaled breath lifted the loose curl from her forehead. She snatched the present from Sam. "You're not off the hook yet. You know you set me up last night."

"Can you save the drama for tomorrow?" Sam said, following her into the living room. "It is Christmas you know."

Kayla perched on the couch and shook the box. "This is too heavy to be a gift card for an online shopping spree." She proceeded to rip open the present.

Sam sat down next to her. "Next time I'll give you a book of coupons."

If her eyes weren't misty, Kayla would have rolled them at Sam. Gently, she lifted the music box with the mahogany base from the packaging. With her fingertips she traced the body of the caramel-colored dark curly haired ice skater striking a pose for an attitude spin.

"Sam, this is beautiful," she whispered. Her eyes remained glued on the figurine.

"And all this time you thought I didn't have good taste," Sam teased. "Check out the music."

With fingertips that suddenly felt numb, Kayla slowly rewound the gold knob. When the instrumental version of "Unforgettable" concluded Kayla leaned into Sam and kissed him on the cheek.

"Thank you," she whispered, still leaning close enough to feel the heat from his breath against her face. "I'll always treasure this. And you," she added after a pause. Her eyes focused on his lips.

Sam's fingertips caressed her cheek. Kayla felt her chin lift, not quite sure if by involuntary muscle movement or assistance from Sam. Before she could figure it out, the warm sensation of Sam's lips pressed against hers.

The kiss ended as quickly as it began. Almost simultaneously, they pulled away and stood up. Kayla still held the music box close to her chest. "Whoa."

"I'm sorry," Sam stuttered. "I wasn't thinking."

Kayla attempted to say something funny to diffuse the situation, but the brief contact rendered her incapable of thinking straight. "We should, um, get going." She pointed to her bedroom. "Let me get my coat." She turned and swiftly headed for her bedroom with the music box still in hand.

Sam slumped down on the couch, rationalizing why he allowed Kayla to kiss him. Or did he kiss her? The kiss she planted on his cheek was soft and sweet, so was her perfume. The rest was hazy. Who initiated the kiss was both unclear and unimportant, it could never happen again. It was a one-time mistake.

"Let's go." Kayla returned with her coat buttoned and purse hanging from her shoulder. She brushed past

Sam and waited for him at the door. "Can you help me carry these?" she asked pointing to the gifts she'd purchased for her family.

"Kayla, we need to talk about what just happened here." Sam stood and walked toward her.

"Why?" she stated. "We both know that little kiss was a mistake and didn't mean anything. Trust me that will never happen again." She held the door open for him. "Come on before we're late. Carlos can be a real monster when he's hungry."

Sam hesitated momentarily before lifting the wrapped gifts and exiting the apartment.

Christmas dinner with the Turners proved to be more than what Sam had anticipated. Travis turned out to be quite intriguing with stories from his days in law enforcement. Carlos placed his misplaced animosity on the back burner for the day. He actually offered his hand to Sam and wished him a happy holiday upon greeting him and Kayla at the front door. Mrs. Turner had prepared a traditional soul food feast which included collard greens, hot water cornbread, and for dessert, banana pudding. Before everyone devoured the feast, Travis said a heartfelt and emotional prayer for grace. Sam realized then Kayla's entire family did not share her opinion about God. Paintings and artwork with religious themes were sprinkled throughout the Turner home. Sam made a mental note to uncover the source of Kayla's anger in the near future.

Sam's reprieve from Carlos was short-lived. At the dinner table, Carlos sat directly across from Kayla and

Sam. Every so often Sam would look up and find Carlos staring at him. Travis and Rozelle were more discreet with their observations.

While still seated at the dining room table, the family exchanged gifts. Travis and Rozelle both received jewelry from each other and gave the children money; for Carlos, a new toy for his truck and Kayla, an online shopping spree. Carlos and Kayla purchased artwork to decorate the walls of the Turners' new home. Carlos kissed his sister's cheek after opening the satellite sound system for his new truck. Listening to Kayla rave over the leather jacket he'd selected for her, Carlos beamed with pride.

"This is wonderful." Kayla walked over and hugged her brother. Rozelle stood and began collecting discarded wrapping paper. "Hold on a minute. I want to show everyone the present Sam got me." Kayla rushed into the living room before Carlos could give Sam the death stare. She returned with a smile that reached the corners of her eyes and the music box in her hand.

Sam didn't know she had it tucked away in her purse the entire time. He assumed she'd left it in her bedroom.

"Isn't this beautiful?" Delicately, she held the treasure out to her mother.

"It sure is," Rozelle agreed. "The skater looks like you." She then turned to Sam. "Where on earth did you find this?"

"Kayla's not the only one who knows how to point and click," Sam teased, at the same time resting his arm around Kayla's shoulder.

Kayla moved closer to Sam. "There's hope for you yet." Kayla winked then turned the gold knob and then closed her eyes as "Unforgettable" filled the dining room.

In Sam's peripheral vision, Carlos' stone-cold face came into focus. All eyes and ears were tuned into the music box. The leather jacket lay folded over a chair.

"The two of you are getting serious," Rozelle commented as she handed the music box back to Kayla.

"We are the best of friends," Sam responded.

Rozelle's face twisted. "Friends?"

"Yes, Mama, just friends."

"Friends?" Rozelle questioned again, this time with her hands on her hips.

"Just friends, Ms. Rozelle. Kayla and I are not interested in anything beyond that." As Sam said the words thoughts of their brief kiss flooded his mind.

Rozelle dropped her hands to her sides. "Since you're just friends you can remove your arm from around her. And Kayla, you can step back and give the man some breathing room. Then you two friends can help me clean the kitchen." She then pointed to Carlos. "You can help too." Rozelle stomped to the kitchen, mumbling something Sam couldn't decipher.

Kayla and Sam laughed at her mother then began clearing the table. No sooner had Kayla carried an arm full into the kitchen, Carlos approached Sam.

"Look, man, my sister likes you. That means I have to tolerate you. So far, you appear to make her happy. I've never seen her so happy. I like the way she smiles and laughs with you." He leaned closer to Sam. "If you make my sister cry, I'll cut you like that spiral ham we just ate." Carlos then smiled and began collecting dishes and whistling "Jingle Bells."

Chapter 8

F rustrated and on edge, Kayla slammed the register drawer closed. If she heard one more manufactured story from a seemingly helpless customer desiring to return an item without a receipt, she'd—she didn't know what she would do, but it wouldn't be pretty.

All morning long, all week as a matter of fact, an endless flow of customers filed into the store. The majority were looking for the after-Christmas sales or needing different sizes. Then there were those who suddenly realized they'd spent too much over the holidays, and then yelled at Kayla when she offered them a store credit. Working retail certainly had its advantages. Being stuck behind the register during the post-Christmas season because two employees called off sick, was not one of them.

Kayla glanced down at her watch and sighed. Ashley should return from lunch any second now. The thought of sitting in her cluttered office at the back of the store eating chicken salad on wheat sounded like a mini vacation from the sales floor chaos.

"Okay, boss, go eat." Ashley returned looking refreshed.

Kayla started to ask the name of her lunch date, but decided not to bother. Chances were he'd be a distant memory in seventy-two hours.

"Is the preacher dining with you today?" Ashley inquired with a hint of mischief. "I haven't seen him in a while."

Kayla sighed heavily. "I'm eating alone today just as I have every day this week. Minister Jerrod volunteers at the Youth Center on Davis Street on Wednesdays." She turned and left before Ashley mentioned Sam again.

Kayla's head hung as she took the long trek to her office. She hated to admit it, but out-of-control customers weren't the sole cause of her irritability. Truth was, she missed Sam. She hadn't seen much of him since Christmas and to make matters worse, she still felt the effects of the brief kiss they'd shared ten days prior. Christmas Day she'd done an outstanding acting job, pretending the kiss was insignificant. In actuality, the encounter connected her to Sam in a way she didn't want to connect with any man.

Thoughts of Sam inundated her to the point he invaded her dreams. Twice she dreamt the two of them were walking on the beach, holding hands. Then there was the one in which they ice skated to "Unforgettable." The nightmare that caused her to wake up screaming, placed her on the front pew inside of a church holding a newborn, encouraging Sam to preach. The baby was hers and Sam's and he was the pastor of the church. After that dream, she stopped listening to the music box at night and tucked it away in the back of her closet. Thinking about it now caused her breathing to accelerate and her palms to sweat.

Mentally drained, Kayla collapsed in her chair. She stared up at the ceiling, in hopes of getting Sam out of her mind. Avoiding him for ten days hadn't helped, why did she think counting the grooves in the ceiling would? She sat forward, resting her elbows on her cluttered desk. Was she avoiding him, or was he avoiding her, or both? They talked to each other every day, but the calls were placed at times when one knew the other had limited time to talk and they jogged at opposite times. He invited her to church on New Year's Eve, but still upset about the play, she declined. He did call her after midnight to wish her a Happy New Year though. She wondered if Sam was spending his time with that woman from the play. It was obvious the woman admired him and she was more suitable for him. The more Kayla thought of them together, sadness gripped her, causing pain in the pit of her stomach. She was bent over when Ashley entered.

"Are you okay?"

Kayla sat up, but kept her arms folded across her abdomen. "I'm fine, I just need to eat."

"Well, hurry up, the police are here to see you."

Suddenly feeling vulnerable, Kayla lowered her head and wrapped her arms around her body. "What do they want?" she whispered.

"They want to talk to you about the..." Ashley couldn't say the last word.

Kayla's eyes watered, but she said nothing.

"If you want, I'll send them away," Ashley offered.

Kayla shook her head. "No. I can't run from reality. Wait two minutes and then escort them back here."

"Are you sure?"

Kayla nodded yes.

Ashley sighed, and then left as quietly as she had entered.

Out of habit, Kayla picked up the phone and dialed Carlos. His phone went straight to voicemail. She punched in Sam's number, but disconnected before the first ring. Sam would never get out of her system if she kept running to him every time fear arrested her. He was probably busy anyway. She placed the receiver back on the base and then fished a tissue from her purse. Kayla decided to face this one alone. She lowered her head and whispered, "Please let this be good news."

After a light knock on the door, two plainclothes policemen entered. She recognized Officer Benson from the hospital. She'd interviewed her after the assault. The other officer, a male, was unfamiliar.

"Good afternoon, Ms. Perez." Officer Benson gestured to her right. "This is Officer James."

Kayla slowly nodded her head in acknowledgment.

"Ms. Perez," Officer Benson continued. "Another assault occurred three nights ago in the parking garage."

Kayla gasped and squeezed the sides of the chair. Her body trembled as flashbacks of that night flooded her mind. She wanted Sam. She needed him to hold her like the day at the marina.

"No need to panic, the assailant has been apprehended and he's no longer a threat to anyone, literally."

Kayla's frantic eyes traveled from one officer to the other. "What do you mean?" she stuttered. Her hands still gripped the chair.

"Since your incident occurred, we planted an undercover cop at Emery Bay," Officer James explained. "Three nights ago, our decoy was attacked while leaving one of the retail stores. Unfortunately for the assailant, his intended victim turned out to be a trained law enforcement officer."

Kayla's involuntary tremors slowly subsided, but she wasn't totally convinced of her safety. "How do you know it's the same guy?"

"Same MO and his bodily fluids matched the samples taken from you." Being unconscious at the time, Kayla didn't remember the specialized exam for victims of sexual assault.

"Aside from that," Officer Benson continued, "he confessed an hour before hanging himself in his cell."

Kayla covered her mouth with her hands to keep from screaming. She rocked back and forth.

"Ms. Perez, I wanted to tell you this personally." Office Benson walked around the desk and placed her hand on Kayla's shoulder. "The assailant was not HIV positive. I thought you'd be relieved to know that."

Kayla's mouth remained covered and tears flowed down her cheeks. She nodded her gratitude.

"Unless you have questions, we'll be leaving. You have my card."

Kayla remained silent.

"One more thing." Officer Benson stopped before reaching the door. "If you haven't done so already, I strongly recommend you get counseling, or join a support group."

Long after the door closed, Kayla sat bent over her desk and released tears of joy and sorrow. Joy, because the perpetrator had been found. Sorrow, because a life was lost. She closed her eyes and a vision of the wooden cross with the stained white fabric flashed. It was the same cross she'd seen at Grace Temple, but something was different. The fabric's movements appeared to beckon her to approach the cross. In her right ear, she heard someone whisper her name. Her eyes bulged open and the tears ceased to flow. She looked frantically around the room. She was alone with her door closed. "This is starting to get spooky," she mumbled. "I'm never stepping foot inside that church again."

~~~

Sam sat at his desk at the Youth Center reviewing the schedule of activities for the upcoming weekend. Danté would love it all: indoor soccer, movie matinee, and a trip to Chuck E. Cheese. Three activities in one day might be excessive, but Sam wanted to spend as much time as possible with Danté. Sam knew all too well how it felt growing up without a father. At least, he had uncles and deacons from the church willing to step in and teach him about manhood and how to respect women. Thanks to his father's disappearing act, Danté's male role models were limited to Sam and the volunteers at the Youth Center.

His motives for hanging with Danté weren't all selfless and for that, Sam repented. He needed someone, or something, anything to distract him from thinking of Kayla. Dodging her hadn't worked and the brief phone calls only fueled his desire to be in her presence. Kayla had become an essential piece to his existence. Why? He didn't know. And what about the kiss? Ten days later, that still puzzled him. Why had he allowed that to happen? The more important question was, why did he enjoy it? He'd prayed on Christmas night for an answer, and every day since. He heard the still small voice clearly, but the response puzzled him: *Just show her Me.* What did that have to do with the kiss? Maybe he made a big deal out of nothing. Kayla certainly wasn't fazed by the episode. He, on the other hand, felt shockwaves every time he thought about the incident. He checked his watch. Two o'clock, the time he normally called Kayla. He lifted the receiver, but before he could dial the number, Bobby Chen Li, the center's director approached his cubicle. He replaced the receiver and gave Bobby his undivided attention. Bobby Chen Li, in his complexity, served as a good distraction.

Sam labeled Bobby as a jack of all religions and a master of none. In the past four years Bobby had professed to be a Jehovah's Witness, fellowshipped with the

Mormons, and currently a practicing Buddhist. He also had an identity problem. He was an African-American, born Leroy Jackson, from Charlotte, North Carolina. Yet his chosen name was Bobby Chen Li. Despite being spiritually confused, Bobby was an outstanding director for the center.

"Sam, I have some news, which I hope is not bad news." He placed a file folder on Sam's desk.

"Shoot."

"Sherri Thomas, Danté's mom, called today."

Sam interrupted. "Is Danté all right?"

"Physically, yes, but she wants us to talk to him about his feelings." Bobby paused. "His father popped up on New Year's Day, stating that he's made a resolution to be a better father. Danté has been withdrawn ever since."

"He's probably terrified," Sam interjected. "I saw the photos. That madman beat him and his mother pretty badly." Sam leaned back in his chair, trying to figure out a way to protect Danté. "Isn't there a restraining order?"

Bobby shook his head. "His mother was too afraid to file one or press charges."

"I don't get it," Sam said, shaking his head. "Why would she let him near her son?"

Bobby hunched his shoulders. "Fear, I guess. Anyway, the guy claims to have changed and is enrolled in counseling."

"I hope it's spiritual counseling."

"So do I. Either way, Danté will be here in an hour for reading. Talk to him, do whatever it takes to prevent this kid from reverting back."

"I'll do what I can, starting now with a word of prayer."

Bobby agreed and joined hands with Sam. Outwardly, Sam prayed for Danté's well-being. Inwardly, he prayed Bobby would stop wandering in the wilderness and surrender his life to Christ.

~~~

Kayla couldn't believe it. Just hours after vowing never to step foot inside Grace Temple again, she found herself standing in the back of the sanctuary in search of a seat for Bible Study. She really hadn't come to learn about the Bible. Kayla wanted to see Sam, but Wednesday was Bible Study night for him. Meaning, he wouldn't return home until late and she couldn't wait that long.

The emotional rollercoaster ride, since learning of her attacker's capture and subsequent death, had taken her through so many loops she'd regurgitated twice. The news had rendered her completely useless. The remainder of the day, Ashley practically ran the store alone, much to the customers' dissatisfaction. For the verbal abuse Ashley endured, Kayla promised her an extra day off with pay.

Her eyes scanned the crowded sanctuary. Throngs of people moved quickly to fill the seats before the seven o'clock start time. Kayla started down the left aisle and strained her neck to see if Sam was down front. She didn't intend to sit on the front row, or any row for that matter. Kayla figured she'd grab Sam just long enough to tell him what happened and then allow his nourishing to soothe her. He'd say the right words, as always, and her world would return to normal. She was too late. The exact moment she reached the third row, Pastor Simmons followed by Sam and other people, who she assumed were clergy, entered the sanctuary from the right side. Pastor Simmons walked onto the podium. Sam and the others sat on the center front row.

Kayla stood motionless and stared at Sam. He looked good dressed in black slacks, white dress shirt, and one of the ties she'd purchased. In his hands was a leather portfolio and ink pen. "What am I going to do now?" she mumbled under her breath. She couldn't walk across the front of the church and drag him off the front row.

"Psst, psst." She attempted to catch his attention, but the volume of numerous conversations made it impossible. She observed Sam until Pastor Simmons addressed the congregation.

"Good evening, church. Please bow your heads."

With all heads bowed, Kayla attempted to make a quick exit. Unfortunately for her, a member tapped her on the leg as she rushed up the aisle and informed her it was inappropriate to walk during prayer.

"Sorry," Kayla mumbled.

"Shush." The woman placed her forefinger to her lips. "And no talking either."

Kayla rolled her eyes and then plopped down in the first available seat the precise moment Pastor Simmons concluded the prayer.

"Tonight our lesson is found in the book of Mark, chapter five," Pastor Simmons began.

Kayla leaned forward and looked in Sam's direction. If he were within striking distance, she would've sucker punched him. This was his fault. If he had come out sooner or better yet, called her this afternoon, she could have gotten what she needed and still made it to bed by eight-thirty. Now here she was stuck in a place she detested with the church warden eyeing her. To make matters worse, she didn't have a Bible to follow along. Kayla didn't own a Bible, not even the pocket-sized one offered free at hospitals and hotels. She started to hold up a finger and tip out, but couldn't remember the correct one.

"Would you like to share my Bible?"

Kayla looked to her right. She'd been too occupied to notice the young woman seated next to her. Kayla opened her mouth to speak, but then decided it was impossible to explain why she was in Bible Study, but didn't believe in the Bible, before the warden came and tapped her hand for talking in church.

"Thank you," Kayla mouthed.

She had planned to give the impression that she was paying attention, but the story Pastor Simmons told compelled her to listen. He talked about a woman hemorrhaging for twelve years and how she'd tried everything and everyone, but none could help her. Pastor Simmons said the woman had great courage and faith to press on to touch Jesus. Kayla listened attentively as he explained how faith and courage were necessary for complete healing in Christ. Near the end of the hour-long lesson, he asked the congregation if they had the courage to admit that they needed healing and the faith to believe that the blood of Jesus heals all wounds.

Soft music played as Kayla pondered the story and what, if anything, did it mean to her. She lowered her head, refusing to look at the wooden cross. The image had invaded her dreams and today she thought she heard it call her name. No way would she look at that cross again. The second Pastor Simmons concluded the benediction, Kayla sprinted toward Sam.

Chapter 9

S am abruptly interrupted his conversation with Tyrell. "Kayla, what are you doing here?"

Kayla stopped within a foot of him. "Hello, Sam, I mean Pastor Jerrod." She then exchanged greetings with Tyrell.

Sam grinned and gestured to embrace her.

Tyrell cleared his throat to catch his attention.

Sam regained his posture. "This is a pleasant surprise. Have you been here the entire time?" "Yes, I—" She nervously glanced at Tyrell.

"I'll meet you in the back," Tyrell said. He then nodded at Kayla. "Nice seeing you again." Sam took her by the hand and led her to the base of the platform. "Kayla, what's wrong?" Sam asked once they were away from the crowd.

"I came here because I needed to talk to you, but I was late and got stuck in Bible Study." Sam chuckled.

"That's not funny. I got stopped by the church police." She told him about the woman she labeled as the warden.

He laughed some more and then became serious. "I'm glad you're here. I hope you enjoyed the lesson."

"We can talk about that later. If you're not busy," she added after a pause.

"Kayla, I'm sorry. I have a meeting with the Youth Department leaders in five minutes."

Kayla looked away in an attempt to hide her disappointment, but Sam saw the sadness. Knowing she needed him caused the muscles in his chest to tighten. Seeing Kayla unhappy made him ache. "Would you like to share dessert with me?"

Kayla faced him. "When?" she asked, suppressing a smile.

"The meeting shouldn't take any longer than twenty minutes. If you provide dessert, I'll stop by."

Kayla was smiling again. "I'll stop by the store and pick up some vanilla ice cream."

"Make it Ben & Jerry's Cherry Garcia and it's a date, or meeting," he quickly added.

"Call it whatever you like, but at least you're spreading your wings." She playfully slapped his arm.

The brief contact reminded Sam of how much he'd missed her, and how much he wished he didn't have to preside over the meeting. "I took your advice. Slowly I'm trying different things and adding more color in my life." Sam reached for his portfolio. "I have to get back to the conference room. I'll see you soon."

Kayla nodded and then watched him turn to leave. "Hey, nice tie," she called to him.

Sam totally forgot he was in a sanctuary full of people. He turned back to her and winked before he said, "A beautiful woman gave it to me." Then he left.

~ ~ ~

Kayla stood there blushing and trying to remember why she'd denied herself the pleasure of his company for so long. She turned to leave and spotted Jasmine a few feet away, staring at her. Kayla nodded in her direction and then headed for the door.

"What kind of church is this?" Kayla said when she saw the bottleneck at the main exit door. "People have to line up to come in and to go out?" The words were meant for her ears only, but the gentleman at the end of the line heard her.

"Pastor Simmons likes to greet the members and visitors on their way out," he explained. Kayla frowned.

"The line moves fast." He interpreted Kayla's frown for impatience. "Pastor shakes your hand and says hello, that's all. He doesn't hold counseling sessions at the door. You need to make an appointment for that."

Kayla smiled before she said, "That's good to know." What would be the point in telling the nice gentleman she didn't want to say two words to Pastor Simmons? She'd only spoken to him the night of the play out of respect for Sam.

She sucked her teeth and moved forward. The gentleman was correct. In less than three minutes, she stood face-to-face with the shepherd of the flock.

Pastor Simmons extended his hand. "God bless you, Sister Kayla. It's good to see you again."

Kayla reluctantly shook his hand. "I'm surprised you remembered my name." She attempted to disengage, but he held onto her hand.

"Don't be. I've been praying for you since the night of the play. If you have any spiritual needs that Pastor Jerrod can't meet, please feel free to call the office and schedule an appointment."

Kayla snatched her hand away. "I don't need anything from you." She then rolled her eyes and stomped away.

Halfway across the parking lot, she regretted her rudeness, but then brushed it off. Pastor Simmons deserved it. He didn't know her and already he offered her special services that would no doubt leave her feeling less than human. "Some things never change," she mumbled before inserting her key into the ignition.

~~~

Sam only knocked once before Kayla swung the door open. Tyrell and the congregation of Grace Temple weren't present, so he stepped inside and enjoyed the embrace he was denied earlier. "Hey, buddy," he said and squeezed her tighter. "I didn't realize how much I've missed you."

"I missed you too," she whispered back. Kayla then broke the embrace and stepped back with her hands on her hips. "Then why have you been avoiding me?" Her neck rolled as she spoke.

Sam closed the door and walked into the kitchen.

Kayla followed behind. "Answer me. Why haven't I seen you in ten days?"

Sam opened the freezer and removed the ice cream. She handed him a spoon.

"Sweetheart, I have been avoiding you for the same reason you've been avoiding me," he said after savoring a spoon of his new favorite ice cream.

Kayla's cheeks flushed. "How did you know?"

Sam dipped the spoon again before answering. "I think we were both caught off guard by that kiss. Although it didn't mean anything to neither of us, we need to set some ground rules so it doesn't happen again.

Relief washed across her face. "I couldn't agree more." Kayla retrieved a spoon from the colander and dipped into the carton.

With his free hand, Sam took her hand and led her to the couch. Kayla sat close enough for her spoon to reach the carton.

"Kayla, I don't know how it happened. I just know it can't happen again. Your friendship means too much to me. I don't want to get caught up again and place myself in a position to compromise what I am saving for my wife."

Kayla's eyes widened.

"Don't look surprised. Women aren't the only ones who believe in purity." He enjoyed another spoonful. "Beyond that, I can't allow my heart to get engaged with someone other than my future wife. The same should hold true for you."

"You're right again, Pastor Jerrod." Kayla slowly savored the ice cream. "Let's make a deal, again." Kayla tucked her legs beneath her. "Name your price."

Sam looked up from the ice cream and gazed into her eyes. "If our feelings change in that either of us desires more than a platonic friendship, we'll end the relationship."

Instead of extending her hand, Kayla ate another spoonful of ice cream, and then held her empty spoon up. "You, my friend, have a deal."

Sam tapped her spoon with his in agreement. Simultaneously, both looked down into the ice cream carton. It was nearly empty.

"Allow me," Sam said then fed her the last of the ice cream. He placed the spoons inside and then sat the carton on the coffee table. He then leaned back with his arm resting on the couch. "Now, what was so urgent that you had to hunt me down in church?"

Kayla's countenance changed from happy to sad. Her eyes watered and her shoulders slumped.

Instantly, Sam sat up and embraced her. "Sweetheart, what's the matter?"

Kayla wiped her face against his dress shirt. If she weren't hurting, he would have reprimanded her for using his shirt as a paper towel.

"The police came to see me today." She sniffled and then continued to tell him everything except the vision of the talking cross.

"How do you feel?"

She was now lying against his chest. "I feel so many things; I don't know which feeling is appropriate. One minute I'm relieved, the next minute I'm sorry he's dead. I wonder if he left a wife and kids and how they feel knowing he killed himself after raping at least two people." She held her head up and looked into his eyes. "Am I wrong to even care?"

He brushed loose curls from her face. "Sweetheart, there's nothing wrong with wondering about the unknown, just don't get stuck there. As cruel as your attacker was, he was still a person and someone loved him. Someone is grieving for him."

"But that person shouldn't be me. I'm the victim here. I'll suffer from his actions for the rest of my life."

Sam stared into her eyes, searching for the best way to approach the subject of Pastor Simmons' message. "Kayla, you don't have to suffer the rest of your life. There is someone who can help you."

Kayla sat up and pulled away from him. "About that story your pastor told tonight. Was that woman really hemorrhaging for twelve years? Why couldn't someone help her? What kind of disease was it anyway? I don't believe that story. No one can experience that for so long and live."

"You're missing the point of the lesson."

"What is the point of someone suffering so long for no apparent reason?"

Sam leaned forward with his elbows resting against his thighs. "Kayla, the point of the story is people suffer for years with both emotional and physical pain. They give the illusion that everything is fine, when in fact, they're dying on the inside. People will try everything and spend a fortune trying to find a cure that only God can provide. He stands with His arms outstretched, waiting for us to come to Him. Once we totally surrender to God's will, He heals all of our wounds, both emotional and physical."

Kayla shook her head from side to side, as if trying to shake something from her memory. "I don't get it. If God is so loving and caring, why does He sit back and watch us suffer? Why does He allow us to hurt when He can help us? And what about children? Bad things happen to children, but they don't understand what it means to have the faith and courage to let Jesus heal them. They carry around all that hurt and then act out with sex, drugs, or even worse." Her voice quivered. "It's not fair. If He's so loving, why does He make us hurt?" Tears rolled down her cheeks.

Sam lifted her chin and forced her to make eye contact. "Kayla, tell me what happened. Why are you so angry with God?"

Kayla shook her head and whispered, "No."

"It's more than your father and the assault, isn't it?"

For an answer she lowered her head on his shoulder and cried.

Sam persisted. "You need to talk about it. Keeping it buried isn't helping you."

"Talking about it didn't help Candace," she snapped and pulled away.

Sam was perplexed. "Who's Candace?"

"Someone I knew a long time ago," she whispered after wiping her eyes. "I'll tell you about her some other time." Sam objected and Kayla interrupted him. "It's late. I have an early day tomorrow."

Sam relented. "Join me for an early morning jog?" If he were going to get her to talk, he'd have to do it on her terms.

"Sure." Kayla stood and stretched. He followed her lead and headed for the door. "Thanks for dessert and the company."

"Next time don't make me come looking for you. Things might get ugly if I have another run-in with the church police." Kayla was laughing, but Sam knew deep down she was hurting. He played along with her.

"You can always sit on the front row next to me."

Kayla rolled her eyes and smacked her lips. "I don't think Ms. Jasmine would like that too much."

He laughed out loud. "I don't believe this. You're jealous of Jasmine. Why, I don't know."

"I am not jealous. I don't have any reason to be jealous, you're just a friend."

His laughter caught in his throat. She said the word friend as if it left a bad taste in her mouth. It also caused uneasiness in his stomach, but he associated the ache with the late-night ice cream. "For the record, I am not interested in Jasmine romantically either," he said, then left.

Chapter 10

Listening to Danté's pleas caused Sam's chest muscles to constrict. His heart ached for the child. How was he supposed to look this innocent child in the face and deny the simple request?

"Please take me with you," Danté pleaded again.

Now more than ever, Sam regretted having mentioned the Youth Snow Trip to Danté. He'd only done so after his mother had signed the permission slip allowing Danté to attend the three-day trip to South Lake Tahoe. If he'd known she would rescind, Sam would have never mentioned it. But he had, and in the process, raised the child's expectations only to have them crushed. Danté's sad and disappointed little face mirrored his own years ago. The few encounters Sam had with his biological father were limited to broken promises and excuses about why he couldn't spend time with Sam. At the age of thirteen, Sam stopped crying about what wasn't and accepted the love and care his uncles offered. He vowed never to neglect his own children.

"I'm sorry, but your father wants you to spend the weekend with him."

Tears drained from Danté's little eyes. "But I don't want to go with him. I want to go with you."

"I know." Sam swallowed the lump in his throat. "I want you to come, but I can't take you if your parents won't allow me."

Bobby Chen Li walked into the math center at the precise moment Danté wrapped his little arms around Sam's leg and screamed, "Please."

"What's going on?" Bobby closed the door to prevent Danté's cries from reaching the other children in the play area.

Sam bent over and lifted Danté into his arms. For Danté's sake he chose his words carefully. "He wants to hang out with me this weekend."

Bobby nodded, indicating he got the message.

Sam rubbed the back of Danté's head until he quieted down and then sat down with him on his lap. Bobby stood beside Sam.

"Danté," Sam began softly, "is your father hurting you again?"

Danté shook his little head from side to side.

"If your father is hurting you, we can help you," Bobby added.

Danté remained quiet while Sam and Bobby checked his back and legs for signs of new abuse. Both men exhaled in relief when no physical evidence was detected.

Bobby squatted down beside him. "Danté, I know how much you like Sam, but you have to obey your parents. Sam will be here when you come back on Monday."

"I'll stop by just for you. I'll even take you to get ice cream," Sam added.

Danté looked into Sam's eyes. "You promise?"

"I promise." Sam answered quickly for Danté's sake. Inside he prayed it was a promise he'd have the chance to keep. He couldn't take anything for granted with the sudden change in Sherri Thomas' behavior. At the last second, she might decide to remove Danté from the Youth Center altogether. Besides canceling the snow trip she'd allowed Danté to spend two of the three afternoons, set aside for reading and math tutoring, with his father.

Danté wiped his face dry. "Okay." Reluctantly, he released Sam and stood to his feet. "Can Ms. Kayla come too?"

"Who is Ms. Kayla?" Bobby asked as he stood to his feet.

"That's his girlfriend," Danté answered before Sam.

Bobby looked at Sam with a raised eyebrow. "Girlfriend? Since when is Pastor Sam allowed to have a girlfriend?"

Sam stood also. "Kayla is not my girlfriend," he declared, while pointing his forefinger at Danté. "We are just good friends."

"Friends, huh?" Bobby smirked then squatted down to Danté's level. "What makes you think Sam has a girlfriend?" he baited.

"Yeah, what makes you think that?" Sam thought he had made his relationship clear to Danté.

Danté looked up at Sam and offered an explanation. "Ms. Kayla is always with you when you pick me up. She went to the park with us and ice skating. And I saw you hold her hand at the movies." Danté paused. "Oh yeah, you call her sweetheart a lot."

Bobby stood to his feet and threw his hands up. "I may be confused about a lot of things, but that sounds like a girlfriend to me." After a hearty laugh, he slapped Sam on the shoulders. "That certainly explains the change in your attire lately. You actually have clothes I wouldn't mind borrowing."

Sam laughed along with Bobby and mentally evaluated Danté's observations. Sure, he'd spent the majority of his free time over the past month with Kayla. They jogged together at least three times a week and shared dinner as often, taking turns cooking. He'd even eaten Sunday dinner with her family, and to his surprise he and Carlos enjoyed a game of one-on-one basketball. As for holding her hand, maybe once or twice, exactly how many times he couldn't remember. As hard as he tried, Sam couldn't remember when the endearing term "sweetheart" became his choice name for her. Was she his girlfriend? At the moment he couldn't adequately answer the question, but he managed to manufacture an answer for the two sets of eyes staring at him.

"Kayla is a girl and she's also my friend. I guess that makes her somewhat of a 'girlfriend'."

"Call it whatever you like, man. I think it's a good thing, just make sure it's a God thing."

Sam watched Bobby's back exit in amazement. Bobby was confused about his identity and spiritual matters, yet he'd managed to hand Sam a reality check.

"Come on." Sam took Danté by the hand. "Let's finish your math homework before your mother returns."

Sam spent the next thirty minutes half-tutoring and half-contemplating his relationship with Kayla. Thoughts of her consumed his mind, causing him to give Danté the wrong answers to two simple addition problems.

"I must also be too old to buy you ice cream," Sam responded when Danté suggested Sam was too old to learn the new stuff.

"No, you're just right."

"Smart kid."

"Ready to go?" Danté's mother entered with a big smile on her face. "Your father is meeting us at the house."

Sam faced the woman, but Danté kept his head down with his lips poked out.

Sherri Thomas walked over to her son and placed her arm around him. "You're not still mad about the snow trip, are you?"

When Danté didn't respond she looked over at Sam with pleading eyes.

Sam uncharacteristically didn't have any sympathy for the woman. In his opinion, allowing Danté to spend unsupervised time with the man who nearly beat him to death, was irresponsible. Sam was a man of integrity. He was not about to help this woman set her son up for a fall.

"See you next week." He rubbed Danté's head and then left the room.

Before he reached his cubicle, his cell phone vibrated on his hip. He retrieved the phone and continued walking down the carpeted hallway. Without checking the caller ID, he flipped the phone open and placed it to his ear.

"Hey, honey. Are you going to Bible Study tonight, or are you coming straight home to pack for the snow trip?"

Sam stopped mid-stride. It was Kayla. Slowly he continued to his workspace and wondered when she'd become comfortable enough with him to use the endearing term. More importantly, why did it sound so good?

"Why do you ask?" he managed after an extended pause.

"I wanted to know what time to have dinner ready or should I leave a plate in the microwave," she answered matter of factly.

Sam collapsed in his chair. When had she become a permanent fixture in his life? He looked down at his attire. Thanks to Kayla he now owned clothing in every color of the rainbow. He even allowed her to talk him into purchasing bright throw pillows and floral arrangements for his apartment. They talked every day, sometimes twice a day, not including the text messages. Kayla made sure he had decent meals. Last month he actually considered buying a Valentine's Day gift for her. Once he'd caught himself fantasizing about how Kayla would look pregnant—with his child. He attributed the thought to the devil and immediately repented. Sam sighed heavily. Danté was right. Kayla was his girlfriend.

"Thanks, but I'm going to Bible Study. I'll pick something up on the way."

"Are you sure? I'm making enchiladas."

Sam chuckled. Kayla knew he had a soft spot for her enchiladas. He wanted to accept, but couldn't. He needed to put some space between him and Kayla and he had to start now.

"I'm sure. Maybe next time," he answered reluctantly.

"Sure," she answered. Her voice deflated and Sam imagined the disappointment in her big brown eyes. "Have a safe trip. Bye."

The line went dead before Sam could change his mind. Disappointing Kayla wasn't something he ever wanted to do, but in order to redefine their relationship, he had to. Having an unsaved girlfriend was not on his agenda.

~~~

Slowly Kayla roamed the aisles of the bookstore, not sure where to look. Normally, she selected her reading material from the supermarket checkout stands or book section at Wal-Mart. Today's purchase wouldn't be a quick read. She'd figured it would take her a lifetime to understand the complexity of its contents and even longer to accept the philosophy. She read the green-and-white overhang sign and smirked. She'd never thought she'd find herself in this section, but over the past month her mind experienced such severe emotional unrest, she didn't have a choice. Pastor Simmons' story invaded her conscious thoughts as well as her dreams. So did visions of that dreaded wooden cross. She visualized the hemorrhaging woman pressing through her crowded retail store and stopping at the register and then asking her for help. At night, the words faith and courage played in her head like an old scratched 45 record. Did she lack courage? Was it necessary to have faith in a God she didn't trust? Should she trust God? Who was God, really? These unanswered questions and more were what brought her back to Grace Temple three weeks in a row on Wednesday nights. She'd sit in the back on the last row. As soon as Pastor Simmons closed his Bible, she'd slip out. Kayla never told Sam about her secret visits for fear he'd take advantage of her interest and preach her a personalized sermon. Her Wednesday night fix was no longer enough, now she needed more. She assumed this was what Pastor Simmons meant by having a hunger and thirst for righteousness. Whatever it was, it led her into the religious section of the major bookstore chain seeking to purchase a Bible.

She didn't know the first thing about selecting a Bible other than she didn't want a translation with all those "Thous" and "saiths." She wanted something easy to read like the one the woman who'd shared her Bible with her that first night had. "Maybe I should have just asked Sam for one of his," she mumbled underneath her breath while surveying the vast selection. She quickly decided that was not a good idea. As it was, she'd allowed herself to become too close to Sam. She realized that this afternoon when Sam declined to have dinner with her. It was bad enough he was leaving her for three days. The least he could have done was share a meal with her before he left. Thinking back on his rejection brought fresh tears to her eyes. Although lighter than the ones she'd shed earlier, they were tears nonetheless and that made her angry. Never in her life had she cried over a man, aside from missing her deceased father and the time Carlos fell from the roof and broke his arm. These tears and the ones she'd shed earlier forced her to face her true feelings toward Sam. The truth she'd known since Christmas morning, but attempted to suppress because the feeling wasn't something she wanted to last, but it had.

Being in love with a minister wasn't on her short- or long-term goal list, but she learned the hard way: The heart has a mind of its own. Sure, she'd made that bogus deal with Sam about not engaging their hearts, but by that time it was too late, she'd already fallen in love. She just didn't know how to tell him without losing his friendship. Today was proof that she needed to put some distance between them. They didn't have a future. She enjoyed charting her own path and didn't have a desire to join Sam on the King's highway. Kayla smirked and thought, then why am I in here buying a Bible? "With or without Sam, me and God have a score to settle," she mumbled then pulled a study Bible from the shelf. She scanned the Table of Contents then thumbed through the pages. It appeared simple enough.

Her steps to the checkout register were quick and light. She glanced down at her watch and decided to drop by Grace Temple to see if the Bible was worth its $75 price tag.

Chapter 11

In less than ten minutes Sam had his wheeled travel bag packed for the three-day snow trip, but in five hours he'd been unsuccessful in removing Kayla from his mind. Not being able to adequately define their relationship frustrated him. What's worse, the seven-year-old child he was supposed to mentor saw what he couldn't or refused to see.

Gnawing at his conscience was the hard-cold fact that honestly, he didn't want their relationship to change. He enjoyed their early morning jogs. Kayla's caramel skin glowed against the burnt sunrise and enhanced her natural beauty. He experienced sheer happiness watching her glide across the ice rink. Their phone conversations and periodic debates stimulated his mind to the point he made excuses to call her often. Her voice was soothing; he even looked forward to her high-drama moments.

"God, what is going on?" he asked audibly. His eyes rolled toward the ceiling in search of an answer. "Why is Kayla in my life? You told me to show her You. I have, but she isn't any closer to receiving Your love than she was five months ago." Sam patted his chest. "I, on the other hand, have grown attached to her. Why?" He stared at the ceiling until the doorbell sounded.

Exasperated, he tossed the travel bag into the corner near the front door. He opened the door without checking the peephole. It was Kayla. One look at her relaxed his tense muscles and brought a smile to his face. Sam studied her. It was after ten o'clock at night, but she wasn't dressed in pajamas. Instead, an oversized sweatshirt and leggings covered her petite frame. Her dark curly hair was pulled back into a ponytail with loose curls hanging down each side of her face which was devoid of makeup. Her fragrance was that of a fresh ocean breeze. In her hand, a purple and white toothbrush.

In that instant all of his questions were answered. Or had he finally acknowledged what he'd been feeling in his heart for weeks? He wasn't sure, but what he felt at that moment was very real. Sam always imagined that the day he fell in love would be a glorious day, but it wasn't. It was a living nightmare. He loved her. He had surrendered his heart to Kayla, a woman who didn't love or respect his God. The love he felt for her could never be expressed or returned. As he stood there, holding the doorknob, his heart loved her and broke at the same time, but he showed no emotion.

"Can I borrow some toothpaste?" she asked with her long eyelashes lowered and pouted lips.

Sam swallowed the lump in his throat. He loved that false innocence she used selectively. "Didn't you borrow a tube three days ago?"

"Yes. See what had happened was," she began then stomped past him into the apartment. "I wanted to see you before you go. Is that a problem?" She plopped down on the couch and grabbed a pillow and squeezed it to her chest.

Sam smiled in an effort to conceal his inner turmoil. He walked over and sat on the arm of the couch with his arms folded. "Of course it's not a problem. But you could have brought me an enchilada, or two as payment."

Without warning, she hit him with the pillow. "You'll have to wait for that. After you turned me down, I decided not to cook at all."

An internal ache filled his heart at the disappointment he saw in her eyes. "Where did you go?"

Obviously, Kayla wasn't ready to tell him about the new black leather book on her nightstand. She simply answered, "Out."

"You spent the evening alone?" Inwardly, Sam scolded himself for the envy that fueled the question.

"No, the place was crowded." She changed the subject before she'd be forced to admit "out" meant sitting in the back of Grace Temple, listening to Pastor Simmons teach on how to pray. She turned her head and pointed to the travel bag.

"I see you're all packed."

Sam wanted to ask more about her whereabouts, but couldn't risk sounding like a jealous boyfriend. "Yeah, we're heading out at the crack of sunlight."

Kayla nervously played with the loose curls. "Too bad Danté had to cancel."

"Yeah."

A pregnant silence filled the room. Kayla twisted the pillow fringes. Sam laced his fingers together to keep from reaching for her hand.

"It's late." Kayla stood and replaced the pillow on the couch then stepped in front of him. Her dark brown eyes locked with his. "I just needed to see you before you left. Be careful. Highway 50 is a tough road this time of year." She then leaned in to kiss his cheek, but at the last second, he turned and their lips met.

Before Kayla could think to turn away, Sam cupped her face with his palms and deepened the kiss. She yielded with complete abandonment.

Sam ended the kiss before the volcano that now controlled his emotions, erupted. He kissed her forehead, closed eyelids, and nose before returning to her lips. With labored breath, he stood and took two steps backward, but maintained eye contact.

Kayla raised her hands to cover her trembling lips. "Sam, I-I, I have to leave," she whispered and then headed out the door, but not before tripping over the chair ottoman.

With tears streaming down his face, Sam leaned his head against the door and locked it. Happy tears mixed with sorrowful ones met at his chin. He'd meant to kiss Kayla the way he had. He couldn't repent for that. He deserved to kiss the woman who held his heart one last time.

Through blurred vision, Sam found his way to his bedroom where he collapsed onto the bed and cried until no tears remained.

He phoned her the next morning while the children loaded their luggage onto the bus. She picked up on the first ring.

"It's me," was all he said in a subdued tone.

"I know," she answered excitedly. "I was hoping you'd call."

Sam sighed after a pause. "We need to talk."

"I thought about what happened all night."

"Me too," he admitted. "Can we talk Sunday evening?"

"Be safe, honey. See you Sunday."

"Bye, sweetheart."

Chapter 12

S am reclined the seat and stretched his long legs. He'd made a good decision in approving the extra funds needed to rent the travel buses for the trip. The coach came equipped with a sound system, DVD player, and a bathroom. All much-needed commodities when traveling with sixty children under age thirteen.

Halfway into the four-hour drive, Sam gave up on enjoying the beautiful snowcapped mountains and Ponderosa pines that outlined Highway 50 and leaned his head against the headrest. He seriously doubted if he'd notice the scenery on the return trip. Perhaps he'd drive up one weekend alone and appreciate the magnificent landscape. All he could think about now was ending his relationship with Kayla.

All night he warred with himself and with God. Why couldn't he marry Kayla? He loved God and as the head of the house, he could take care of the spiritual needs until she came around. He could fast and pray until she surrendered. After all, she wasn't a morally bad person. God had placed Kayla in his life. Why had He done that, knowing he would fall in love with her? Individuals professing to love Jesus married the unsaved all the time, why couldn't he?

To whom much is given, much is required. The still small voice quieted his ranting. Sam repented to God, but his heart remained hungry for Kayla. Then the thought occurred to him that Kayla didn't share his feelings. The trepidation in her eyes after the kiss was evidence of that. He was in love with a woman who didn't love him in return. Sam thought of Camille and moaned. This is how she must have felt when he delivered the news that broke her heart. Reaping was hard. He moaned again.

"Now are you ready to tell me what's going on?" Tyrell's voice beside him interrupted the pity party. "You've been moping the entire ride and now you're adding sound effects. What happened with Kayla?"

Too drained to question how his friend knew his solemn disposition involved Kayla, Sam answered, "Nothing. Everything."

Tyrell leaned forward. "Everything?"

"Not everything. I haven't been intimate with her. At least not physically," he mumbled.

"Oh." Tyrell returned to his relaxed position. "You must have finally realized that you're in love with her." He causally made the statement as if he were commenting on a basketball game.

It was Sam's turn to lean forward. "Since you're so smart, why didn't you tell me?" His voice rose.

"Man, calm down. I've been trying to tell you since Christmas Eve, but you weren't listening. You've been too busy color-coordinating your wardrobe and cooking cinnamon French toast to hear anything."

Sam shook his head. "You could have tried harder."

"Oh, really?" Tyrell smirked. "Every time I voiced my concern, you had the perfect theological answer: 'I'm praying about it.' You should have stopped praying and listened to what He had to say."

"Whatever, man." Sam waved the true comment off and resumed his leaning position.

"So what are you going to do about it?" Tyrell asked a quarter mile down the road.

"The only thing I can do." Sam answered with false confidence. "The feeling isn't mutual. Even if it were it wouldn't matter. She still hasn't accepted Christ and a relationship with me wouldn't bring about a genuine conversion."

Tyrell nodded his understanding of his friend's dilemma, but didn't comment.

Sam sighed in frustration. "Tee, man, if it weren't for the salvation thing, she'd be perfect. She's everything I desire—drama and all. What if—"

"Man, don't go there." Tyrell cut him off. "You have a divine calling on your life to one day lead God's people. Don't let your emotions cause you to forfeit your destiny. I'm not suggesting your feelings for Kayla aren't real. I know you love her, I've seen it for weeks. But the plain hard truth is, you can't serve two masters."

Sam perched forward and retorted, "Serving the Master is what got me into this mess. I prayed for a wife and then in walked Kayla Perez. He's the one who placed her in my life and told me to be gentle with her."

Tyrell remained calm. "But did He tell you to fall in love with her?"

Deflated, Sam leaned back and mumbled the answer. "No. I thought I could control my heart."

"Humph. You know what the Bible says about the heart being deceitful." Tyrell patted his friend on the back. "Maybe Kayla is the one God has for you, but not at this time. If the two of you are meant to be, God will reunite you at the proper time." Tyrell paused. "But in the meantime, you know what you must do."

"Yeah." Sam turned his face to the window and remained in that position the rest of the ride.

Chapter 13

"You went where today?" Carlos asked for the second time. "I must be hearing things."

Kayla spun around and glared at her brother, sitting at her kitchen table. "Don't act like I've never been inside of a church before? We used to go when we were little, remember?" That was the best way she could explain why she woke up with the desire to attend Grace Temple on a Sunday morning.

"Mija, Christmas was three months ago and Easter is three weeks away." Carlos folded his arms across his chest. "And let's not forget, you detest church with a passion."

"Whatever." Kayla rolled her eyes at him and then continued preparing dinner. "I bought a Bible too," she added over her shoulder. "And I have been attending Bible Study."

Carlos perched forward. "Wow. Sam got you to convert."

She dropped the spoon she stirred the meat with on the floor. "He did not," Kayla defended after retrieving the utensil. "For your information, he doesn't know about church or Bible Study. This is all my doing." She wanted to add, "With the urging of that psychotic cross," but didn't. Her brother would think she was crazy for sure.

"How can he not know? You're always together."

"We're not always together."

Carlos narrowed his eyes and twisted his lips.

Kayla threw her hands down in resignation. "Okay, maybe we are together most of the time, but on Wednesdays I sit in the back and leave before dismissal. I just bought the Bible four days ago."

He leaned back and stretched his legs. His thumb and forefinger massaged his chin. "What?"

"Mija, you really care about Sam, don't you?"

Kayla was unsuccessful at preventing the huge smile that spread across her face. "I'm in love." The smile remained after she wiped the tears that trickled down her cheeks. "I tried so hard to keep it from happening, but it's no use. I really love him."

"Does he feel the same?"

She reflected on the kiss four days ago. "He hasn't verbalized it, but his actions show it."

Carlos joined her at the stove and embraced her. "I'm happy for you, mija. For the record, I like Pastor Sam Jerrod, but don't let him know that."

"I haven't told him yet," she said between sniffles, "so don't go babbling to Mama."

He released her. "Your secret is safe with me for twenty-four hours. I can't guarantee anything after that."

"That's enough time for me to tell Sam; he'll be here in a couple of hours." She walked over to the sink and washed her hands. "I'm making enchiladas for him."

"Can a big brother get a morsel to eat? Or is everything for your man?"

Her cheeks flushed. The thought of Sam being her man warmed her. "Give me twenty minutes, and I'll make you a plate, but eat fast. I have a date. On second thought, I'll pack your plate to go."

Two hours later Kayla nervously paced her apartment in anticipation of Sam's arrival. Everything was in place. She didn't have much experience in the romance department, but hoped the scene she created was an adequate atmosphere for the transitioning of their relationship from friendship to one of a romantic nature. The table was set with apple cider chilling in the ice bucket since Sam didn't drink alcohol. Soft jazz music permeated from the sound system and scents of lavender filled the air. As for her apparel, in celebration of spring, she selected canary Capri pants with a matching tunic. White two-inch sandals showed off her fresh pedicure.

Once again second thoughts filled her mind about expressing her true feelings to Sam. What if they weren't compatible? She quickly dismissed the anxious thought. Unofficially, she and Sam had been companions for months. Compatibility was not the issue. However, there was that church-thing issue, which she rationalized, could be resolved with compromise. She wouldn't interfere with his religious life, if he didn't pressure her. Who knows, one day she may even join church.

After today's service, Sunday morning worship at Grace Temple was a possibility. With Sam away with the youth, she didn't have to hide in the back. Kayla sat seven rows from the front on the left side to avoid having an obstructed view of the wooden cross. Much to her surprise she enjoyed Praise and Worship and the choir. Now that she could follow along with her Bible, she found Pastor Simmons intriguing to the point she took a few notes. She still hadn't grasped the whole prayer thing, but every day Sam was away, she prayed in her own way for his safe return.

She returned to the kitchen and removed the salad from the refrigerator. While adding the salad dressing, she pondered the best way to profess her love for him. Should she say it the second she opened the door or wait until after the meal? "Maybe I should write him a love note?" she said out loud. Before she seriously considered the idea, the doorbell rang. Too late.

~~~

"Father, help me to follow You and not my heart. Help me not to lean to my own understanding and allow You to work." With his palms against the wallpaper, Sam leaned against the wall outside Kayla's apartment and prayed for the courage to clean up the mess he'd made of his life.

For three days he prayed for an alternate solution to ending his relationship with Kayla. There wasn't one if he regarded the Bible as God's word. He did, and didn't expect God to alter the scripture for his sake. As a servant of God, he could not be unequally yoked in marriage with a non-believer. He wasn't the prophet Hosea and God didn't give him that charge.

That didn't dissolve the love he felt for Kayla. He hadn't ended the relationship yet, but his body was going through withdrawal. Throbbing headaches plagued him the duration of the snow trip. His healthy appetite, replaced by grief and mourning. At night he tucked his head inside his sleeping bag and cried private tears for what could have been.

Tyrell allowed him space, but on the return trip home reminded him that if it was God's will for he and Kayla to be together, eventually it would happen. Sam sighed now as he did then and accepted the finality.

In slow motion, his hand moved from the wall to the doorbell. His finger trembled as he pressed the bell.

"Hey, you." Kayla stepped forward and wrapped her arms around his neck. "I missed you."

He returned the embrace, but held her longer than normal, savoring her feel and scent. "I missed you too." He raised his head to meet her eyes. "You look beautiful."

"Thank you." She pulled away, but interlocked her hand with his and started for the kitchen. "I hope you're hungry. I made enchiladas."

After closing the door he started to follow her then suddenly changed his mind. If he didn't do this now, he doubted if he ever would.

"Wait," he said and gently squeezed her arm. "There's something I need to tell you."

Slowly she turned to face him. "Okay." She led him to the couch.

Once seated, Sam turned to face her. The sight of her smile sent a sharp ache through his chest.

"I'm listening."

"Kayla," he massaged her hand as he talked. "You're the most extraordinary woman I have ever met. You're strong, intelligent, beautiful and a great friend." He paused and drew a deep breath. "I'm sure after what happened the other night, you are aware my feelings for you have changed."

"Yes," she said softly and slowly.

"Because of that some changes must be made."

She squeezed his hand to indicate she understood his meaning. "I know."

Sam swallowed hard then gathered both her hands to his mouth. Gently, he kissed them individually. He recaptured her eyes. "Kayla, I am in love with you."

Her eyes instantly pooled. "Sam, I—"

He placed a finger to her lips to quiet her. "Please, this is not easy for me. Let me finish."

She nodded and he removed his finger.

"I didn't mean to fall in love with you, but I did. And I have to take responsibility for that. This is the hardest decision I have ever had to make."

Kayla looked perplexed.

"I'll always cherish our time together, but we can no longer be in a relationship of any kind."

Kayla blinked her eyes and shook her head as to clear it. "What?"

"It's not you. It's me. I can't be just your friend any-more," he explained. "I love you too much."

"Then why not take our relationship to the next level, instead of ending it?"

It was then Sam realized that Kayla didn't understand his position. He searched his mind for the right words to explain why the two of them could not unite as a couple.

"As a minister, I date for the single purpose of find-ing the woman God has ordained for me, for marriage. You are not a Christian; therefore, I cannot date you. I cannot marry a woman who's not devoted to Christ."

For what seemed like an eternity, a blank gaze veiled Kayla's hot-red face. She didn't blink or breathe. Sam watched as her chest began to heave. Then a piercing wail from deep within her spirit erupted and saturated the entire apartment.

"Why does God hate me so much?"

The cry caught Sam off guard. "Huh?"

Without warning Kayla ran to the CD player and pressed the power button off. "Why can't God love me the way he loves everyone else?" she screamed at him.

Sam stood to his feet, totally confused. "God does love you. He loves everyone."

"No, He doesn't." Her head shook rapidly. "He picks those He wants to love and protect. The rest of us, people like me, He gives us nothing, but heartache and pain."

He attempted to close the distance between them, but she held her hands up. "Kayla, what are you talking about?" She began pacing back and forth in front of the couch with the ravings of a madwoman.

"I'm talking about your God. The same God that has taken everything dear to me away."

"Sweetheart, calm down."

"Don't tell me to calm down," she screamed. "And don't call me sweetheart. You just dumped me because I'm not holy enough for your God."

The crazed looked in her eyes scared him. Her actions superseded that of a drama queen. The pacing continued at a faster speed. Sam began praying audibly for her. "Father, grant Kayla peace and comfort—"

Before he completed the sentence Kayla yelled, "Maybe He will hear your prayer, because He never answers mine."

"God always answers the prayers of His children," Sam defended.

She threw her hands up. "My point exactly. I'm not good enough to be one of His children."

"That's not true—"

She stopped pacing long enough to glare at him. "Be quiet and listen."

He complied without protest.

She resumed pacing.

"When I was three years old your wonderful loving God took my daddy away from me. I have longed for my father's presence all my life, but all I can remember about him is the nickname he gave me. Do you know how hard it is for a girl to grow up without her daddy to validate her?" She didn't wait for him to answer. "Of course not, God is your father."

Sam flinched at the sarcasm, but didn't interrupt.

"And look at what He did to Candace. We grew up together like sisters. We had dreams of joining the Olympic figure skating team and winning gold medals. Then get married and have two kids, a boy and a girl." Kayla wiped tears from her chin. "None of that happened because at age fourteen a man she trusted repeatedly molested her. She wouldn't tell anyone but me. When she became pregnant, I went with her to tell her mother, but her mother didn't believe us." Her voice quivered, but she continued to pace. "Her mother called us evil liars and told us we were going to hell for slandering the man of God. See, the man who stole her innocence was their pastor. The child molester was holy, and we were the wicked ones. After her mother kicked her out the house, Candace lost her will to live. She slit her wrists the day before her fifteenth birthday. Why would a loving God allow that to happen?" She stopped abruptly and cried openly.

Sam held her tightly against his chest and allowed her to completely release years of suppressed emotions. Finally knowing the source of her resentment toward God overwhelmed him to the point he shed tears of his own.

"I'm not finished." She stepped from the embrace, but instead of pacing she leaned against the entertainment center. "If your God loved me, he would not have allowed a stranger to rob me of my virginity and then discard me like day-old garbage. I don't do drugs or participate in risky behavior, but I lived with the fear of being infected with HIV." She locked eyes with Sam. "Your wonderful loving God didn't protect me."

Sam moved his mouth to speak, but once again she held her hand up to stop him.

"Funny thing is, I have actually been trying to better myself so He would love me."

Sam looked perplexed.

"I've been attending Bible Study on Wednesday nights."

"Where?" Excitement spilled over.

"Grace Temple. I sit in the back and leave before dismissal. I even bought a Bible the other day, so I can try to figure out what I'm not doing right. I went to church this morning."

"Kayla, that's wonderful."

"No, it's not," she said, shaking her head. "He just took someone else I love from me."

"Who?"

"You. I love you, Sam. Or should I say, Holy Pastor Jerrod."

He gasped.

"I was going to tell you that tonight before you reminded me that I'm not fit for God's kingdom."

Pain and regret enveloped Sam and caused him to fall to his knees. Thick tears streamed down his cheeks. "Kayla, that's not true. God loves you and so do I."

"I know. He loves me immensely." She walked and stood over Sam. "That's why He told you to break my heart." She continued to the front door and held it open. "Pastor Jerrod, you should leave now. I'm sure there are some people worthy of God's love waiting for you."

Sam maneuvered upright and attempted to reach for her. "Kayla, let's talk about this."

"No, I'm tired." She moved beyond his reach. "I don't have anything left. This morning when I woke up, I was happy because I was in love and I knew you loved me in return. You never said it verbally, but after that kiss, I knew. And now it's over." She paused to wipe her face. "Thank you for helping me through the hard times. After I close the door behind you, I don't want to see you or talk to you. Please don't call me and adjust your routine so our paths won't cross."

"Kayla, don't do this," he pleaded.

"I didn't, you and your God did."

Sam stood there and openly wept. Kayla offered no comfort or compassion, just the cold hallway. He lowered his head then left her apartment for the final time.

Chapter 14

Kayla abruptly dropped the armload of sundresses on the floor and ran from the sales floor to the stockroom. She made it inside the bathroom just seconds before the contents of her stomach erupted. She'd skipped both dinner last night and breakfast this morning. What remained was a bitter-tasting liquid that equaled the bitterness covering her heart. As she watched the yellow substance circle the toilet bowl, she wished she could disappear into the sewage system along with it.

Depression and anger fiercely fought her mind and spirit all night long. During the moments her anger subsided, she cried hot tears for everything she'd lost: love, trust, hope, peace and joy. Then anger ravaged her with a vengeance. She cursed the day she met Sam and the church. Her bedroom was decorated with particles from the music box she'd slammed against the dresser. Her floor, littered with shredded pages from her newly purchased Bible.

The more she raged out of control the more she hurt. Her head pounded, her muscles ached and her vision blurred. She felt her body shutting down and wished death would consume her. Maybe if she died and returned as a different person, her life would be better. Slowly, consciousness seeped from her as she fell to the floor. Carlos found her that way, on her bedroom floor in the fetal position.

Now leaning over the toilet, she shuddered thinking what would have happened if her brother hadn't stopped by on his way to work for more enchiladas. And what if he didn't have a spare key? But he did and like always, her big brother came to her rescue.

After shaking her awake and helping her clean her face, Carlos forced her to tell him what happened.

"Mija, I'm so sorry," he whispered in her ear while he held her. "I know how much you wanted this."

"What's so wrong with me?" she whimpered.

"Nothing is wrong with you. Trust me, this is Sam's lost." Carlos cleaned up the mess while she showered and then drove her to work. "Mija, don't let this get the best of you. You are a beautiful woman worthy of the greatest love," he told her before driving off. Kayla still didn't believe that.

"Kayla, are you okay?" Ashley opened the stall door. "You're not pregnant, are you?"

She slowly stood and ripped tissue from the roll. Kayla wiped her face before she rolled her eyes at Ashley. "I'll be fine."

"You don't look so good. Maybe you should see a doctor?"

Kayla exited the stall and staggered over to the sink and rinsed her mouth without looking at her reflection in the mirror. She didn't need conformation; Kayla knew she looked like death with her red and swollen eyes. That's exactly how she felt. "I'll be fine, just give me a few minutes."

"Do you want me to call Sam? At least he can pray for you, if you refuse to see a doctor. I would pray, but I have backslidden so far, I'd have to show Jesus my ID for him to recognize me."

Kayla stood erect and glared at Ashley. "If you intend to continue working here, don't mention Samuel Jerrod or God again."

Ashley's jaw fell.

Without another word Kayla slammed the bathroom door.

~~~

Sam lifted the spoon to his mouth for the third time. Like the previous attempts he missed his mouth and spilled oatmeal onto his tie. Kayla's tie, one of the few things he had left to remember her by. This time he didn't bother wiping the hot substance from the silk fabric. What was the point in being clean on the outside when on the inside he felt dirty for hurting Kayla? He stared around his church office. The walls displayed his degrees and recognition certificates. The six-shelf bookcase overflowed with Bibles and reference books. On his desk next to a photo of his mother lay his favorite Bible.

Wanda B. Campbell

At the moment none of that meant anything to him. God had deceived him, and in the process caused him to hurt the only woman he ever loved.

If only he'd known about the major steps Kayla had made. If only he'd sat in the back once in a while, he would have noticed her. He could have accompanied her to the bookstore and helped her select a good study Bible. Instead of going out, they could have studied scripture.

"I don't understand," he told Tyrell on a 2:00 a.m. call. "I prayed constantly for her, why didn't God reveal her growth to me? Instead of breaking her heart, I could have helped her in so many ways."

"Maybe God wants her to accept Him without you dangling over her head as the grand prize." Tyrell clarified further. "It's no doubt that God placed you in her life, but consider your role. Maybe your role was to plant the seed and add the water to help her grow. Now could be the time for Kayla to seek after God on her own, so He can give the increase."

"But Tee, she loves me and I love her. Why can't we grow together?" Sam whined.

"If, and only if it's God's will, the two of you will unite. Until then you have to trust that our Father knows exactly what He's doing," Tyrell said with finality.

Exasperated now at his desk, Sam blew out hot air with such force that oat flakes leapt from his tie onto his desk calendar. He didn't bother cleaning them. His friend's words sounded good, but they stopped short of easing the pain in his heart. Twenty-four hours hadn't passed yet and he missed his friend so much he'd lost hand-eye coordination. Just as he reached across his desk for a tissue, his door swung open with such force the doorknob scraped the paint from the wall. Carlos stood in the doorway, nostrils flaring with fists at his sides.

Sam froze with his arm stretched across the desk. His breath caught in his throat, causing his mouth to hang open.

"I warned you about hurting my sister," Carlos snarled.

Sam forgot the oats and brown sugar affixed to his tie and inwardly prayed for divine intervention to prevent Carlos from disturbing the other church staff members. In his high school days he fought with the big, bad and ugly. But after last night, he had nothing left. If Carlos wanted to beat him until his own mother couldn't recognize him, he wouldn't resist.

Sam held eye contact and stood upright. "Look, if you want to cripple or maim me, go right ahead." He held his arms wide open. "You can't hurt me anymore than I have already hurt myself."

"Don't bet on it." In four long quick strides Carlos walked around the desk and stood in Sam's face. He glared down and blew his hot breath directly into his eyes.

Sam didn't blink or flinch. Just in case Carlos succeeded in sending him to an early grave, Sam inwardly repented for every sin he'd committed and for being angry with God.

Carlos drew his right fist back, but stopped short of making contact with Sam's jaw. "Do you love my sister, or not?" he yelled.

Slowly, he released oxygen. "Yes, I do love Kayla."

Carlos lowered his fist. "Then why does she look like death twice over?"

Sam plopped back down into his chair to massage the ache in his chest, but had forgotten about the oatmeal. The slimy substance seeped between his fingers. "Is she okay?" He waited for the answer before finally cleaning his fingers.

"What do you think?" Carlos smirked. "She's angry and depressed. In a matter of hours she went from reveling in the euphoria of love to waddling in worthlessness."

Sam placed his head in his hands and cried. "I never meant to hurt her. I didn't plan to fall in love with her, but I did."

Carlos walked back to the front of the desk and planted his fist on the base. "If you love her so much—which I'm convinced of since you're sitting here crying like a wimp—then why did you toss her aside like that dirty tissue?" He gestured toward the crumbled paper.

Sam grabbed more tissue and wiped his eyes. "You may not understand, but as a minister, I can't be romantically involved with someone who doesn't believe in God. I didn't know Kayla had changed her stance. I wouldn't have ended our relationship had I known."

Carlos shook his head from side to side. "Sounds like you were too busy focusing on the fact that she doesn't love God. Did it ever occur to you to just love her until she found God?"

Sam's head snapped up.

"I don't know much about church and relationships, but what if God was using your relationship to soften her and to show her that all is not bad in the church?" Carlos exhaled and ran his hand though his thick hair. "I don't know what Kayla's told you, but she's not an evil person. She's very loving and caring. It was that thing with Candace that changed her."

"She told me about that."

"And you still dumped her?" Carlos asked incredulously.

"That was before I knew?"

Carlos paced the length of the desk. Kayla and her brother expressed frustration in the same manner, Sam observed.

Carlos threw his hands up. "Look, Reverend Minister Pastor, or whatever you call yourself, wait a few days and I'll talk to her."

Sam's eyebrows narrowed, but before he could ask Carlos why he made the offer, Jasmine stood in the doorway.

"I heard a noise earlier; is anything wrong?" Her eyes alternated between the two men, but lingered on Carlos.

"We're fine for now," Carlos answered without taking his eyes off Sam. "You'll hear from me in a few days." Carlos then turned to leave. "In the meantime, you need to pray or whatever it is you do, so you can make things right with Kayla."

"Thank you," Sam called out.

Carlos stopped and faced Sam again. "Don't thank me. I'm not doing this for you. Make no mistake about it, I don't care if you're happy or not. But I love my sister and the only time she's happy is when she's with you. And deep down, I believe you do love her. You look just as miserable as she does." Carlos paused in the doorway.

Jasmine momentarily stared at him then finally moved.

"Sam, who is that?" she asked once Carlos was out of earshot.

"Carlos. Kayla's brother," Sam answered with his head still lowered.

Jasmine moved her mouth to say something. "I'll be back," she said before running out.

Chapter 15

Kayla yielded to her exhaustion and eased down on the bed in her mother's spare bedroom. Freefalling would have taken what little breath she had left away. Six o'clock in the evening and she still hadn't eaten. The nausea subsided, but her appetite remained a distant memory. Energy sapped and the desire to live gone, she wanted nothing more than to climb into her bed and submerge herself under the covers, but Carlos suggested, more like demanded, she visit their mother.

"Mom's a woman; she can help you get through this," is what he'd said during his afternoon call. "She knows what it's like to have a broken heart."

Kayla was too weak to argue and complied without protest. Maybe her mother did have the cure to mend her brokenness. As a child, she could always count on Rozelle to conjure up a remedy for physical ailments. One teaspoon a day of cod liver oil was the cure for everything from the common cold to diarrhea. Cocoa butter caused all scars to magically disappear. Chicken noodle soup relieved constipation and ice cream cooled heartburn. Kayla hugged the pillow and squeezed her eyes shut. If only she could go back to that day at the marina when Sam held her on the bench. Then she felt cherished and secure. She turned onto her left side and tried to imagine her father's arms around her, but remembrance of Sam's touch interfered with her manufactured memories. She didn't remember her father. If Kayla had the energy she would have pretended the pillow was Sam's face and punched him unconscious. Instead, she slapped the pillow.

"Baby, sit up and eat some of this soup." Rozelle entered, carrying a plastic tray.

Slowly Kayla sat up and positioned her back against the headboard. "Mama, I don't want to eat," she whined.

"You have to eat. Carlos said you haven't eaten all day." Rozelle placed the tray on her lap. "If you don't, you're going to make yourself sicker." She scooped a spoonful of soup and lifted it to Kayla's lips. "Open up."

Reluctantly, Kayla obeyed and after swallowing turned her head and groaned. "I don't want anymore."

Rozelle sighed and set the tray on the nightstand. "Are you ready to tell me what's wrong? The only thing your brother would say is that you and Sam broke up. Which is really funny because I thought the two of you were just friends?"

Kayla rolled her head toward her mother. "Ma, you didn't believe that crap on Christmas, don't pretend you do now."

"I don't." Rozelle smirked. "That man has been smitten with the Kayla bug since the first day he met you. What I don't know is why that changed."

"According to him, it hasn't. He says he loves me," Kayla whispered.

"Do you love him?"

Kayla stared up at the vaulted ceiling and willed her emotions to change, but her heart wouldn't cooperate.

"Yes."

"Then what's the problem? Why are you starving yourself?"

She continued to stare at the ceiling, this time in search of the best way to avoid having this conversation about what she believed or didn't believe concerning God with her mother.

"Well?"

"Ma, Sam dumped me because I don't believe in God." Tears welled in her eyes.

"Come again."

Kayla cleared her throat. "Sam is a minister and will one day pastor a church. The woman he marries has to at least know how to get a prayer through."

Rozelle pointed a finger in Kayla's face. "Why do you keep saying that? You learned about God as a child. I admit, we didn't attend service every Sunday, but this family believes in God and Jesus born of the Virgin Mary."

Kayla used the back of her hand to wipe her cheeks. "Mama," she tried to explain. "You believe in God, but I don't. At least, I don't think I do."

"Kayla Alicia Perez, what are you talking about? You come from generations of good God-fearing Christians. My family is loaded with Baptist, Pentecostal, and Methodist believers. Your father may not have followed all the teachings to the letter, but he was Catholic. He went to Mass every Sunday that he was sober. I have baptismal papers with your name on them that declare you're a Christian."

"Mama, please."

"Please, what? All this talk about not believing in God is casting a dark cloud over this house. I don't want God's blessings to skip over me because of your nonsense."

Fresh tears fell as dread and depression took up residence once again in Kayla's spirit. No longer was she afraid of God taking his wrath out on her, now she had to consider the negative impact on her family. The evil pronouncement by Candace's mother from years ago rang in her head. Was God so cruel that he would make her mother suffer for giving birth to an evil hellion?

Rozelle handed her the paper towel from the tray. "Baby, where is all this coming from?"

Kayla's heavy heaving was her answer.

Rozelle hugged her daughter close to her bosom and rubbed her head. "Baby, tell me. What is it?"

"Mama, why does God hate me?"

Rozelle stopped rubbing. "Baby, God doesn't hate you. He loves you."

Kayla's head shook against Rozelle's bosom. "No, He doesn't. He hates evil and I'm evil. That's why bad things happen to me."

Rozelle rocked from side to side. "Baby, I know the rape was traumatic, but—"

Kayla cut her off. "It's not just the rape. It's my whole life."

Rozelle ceased rocking. "Kayla, talk to me." She quietly listened to her daughter poor out years of confusion and pain. From her misguided view of her father's death to Sam's rejection. She knew Candace's death was devastating for Kayla, but never imagined the events that led up to the child's suicide. She assumed Candace had caved into usual teenage peer pressure, not the unnatural affections of a sinful preacher. And under no circumstances did she ever think her daughter had been condemned to hell.

Rozelle squeezed her tightly. "Baby, I am so sorry you have carried all those lies for so long."

"Mama, it's true. All of it." Her tears soaked Rozelle's dress.

Rozelle lifted Kayla's head and locked eyes. "You listen to me. None of that is true. God didn't take your father's life because you're evil. Your daddy died because he wouldn't stop drinking. We argued all the time about his excessive drinking and driving. Then one Friday after cashing his payroll check, he decided to celebrate at a local bar and then got behind the wheel and wrapped his truck around a telephone pole. That had nothing to do with you. Your father gambled with his life one too many times and lost."

Confusion veiled Kayla's face. This was the first time she'd heard of her father's drinking habit. Rozelle always highlighted the good.

As if reading her mind, Rozelle continued. "Overall, your father was a good man, but his selfishness robbed me of a husband and you and Carlos of a father. After his death I refused to trust a man with my heart. That's why it took so long for me to remarry. I was afraid Travis would leave me in the same position, alone with a broken heart. Thank God that man had the patience to convince me otherwise." Rozelle sniffled and wiped the lone tear that slid down her cheek. "Now as for Candace; Evelyn was wrong for what she said. You and Candace were not evil, the man that molested and impregnated her daughter was. But she couldn't allow herself to see it until it was too late. In her heart, I believe she knew the truth. Shortly after Candace's death, there was a scandal at her church involving her pastor and a thirteen-year-old girl. Not long after his firing, Evelyn lost her mind. She's been living in a state mental institution ever since. The last time I visited, she asked me to find Candace and bring her back so they could be a family again. That was almost ten years ago. I just couldn't bring myself to go back."

Kayla laid her head back in her mother's bosom. With the truth came clarity, but also carried pain.

"I don't know why that man assaulted you, but I know it wasn't because you're evil. And as for Sam, based on the information you've shared, he did what he thought was best for a man in his position. To be honest, I agree with him. A preacher can't be unequally yoked. But this is the perfect opportunity for you to find God, exclusive of Sam. Now is the time for you to build a personal relationship with God and learn more about him. And if it's God's will, you and Sam will reunite."

Kayla pulled away from her mother. "No, Mama, I don't want Sam anymore and I'm not ready to get acquainted with God, at least not today." She stood and reached for her purse. "Thanks, Ma, you've helped me put some things in perspective, but I need to be alone right now."

"Kayla!" Her mother called to her as she left the room. When Rozelle reached the living room Kayla was gone.

New revelations pounded Kayla's mind on the ride home. What if her father was a victim of his own unwise decision and not the casualty of an unjust God? Knowing of Evelyn's remorse, didn't remove years of condemnation. Instead of resolution, more animosity plagued her. If God cared about her, why had He allowed her to suffer unfairly all these years? Why didn't He reveal the truth to her sooner? Pulling into her assigned spot in the parking garage, she quit trying to figure God out. It didn't matter anymore. If He loved her fine, if not, that was fine too. As of tonight, she was going to stop missing what she never had.

The next morning, shortly after 7:00 a.m., her phone rang. Assuming it was her overbearing brother, she answered without checking the caller ID. "Don't worry, I'm feeling better and I promise to eat today."

"I'm glad to hear that because I just placed a tray outside your door."

She gasped at the sound of Sam's voice.

"I would have knocked, but I was afraid you wouldn't answer."

Butterflies danced in her stomach at the sound of his voice. She didn't want to feel connected to him. "You're right," she sternly replied. "I thought I told you not to call me." She heard him sigh on the other end.

"Kayla, I'm sorry I hurt you, but know that I do love you and I want the best for you."

"Did you run that by God?" she snapped. "He might have a problem with a holy man like you affiliating with a heathen like me."

"Kayla, please don't say things like that."

"I won't say anything." She slammed the phone down and then headed for the front door. She opened the door and found a covered tray with cinnamon French toast, bacon, scrambled eggs, and sliced fruit. She shot daggers at Sam's apartment before carrying the tray inside and devouring its contents.

Chapter 16

S am sat at his cubicle and reviewed the list of activities for the upcoming weekend. Thanks to the generosity of the local NBA basketball team, the entire Youth Center had prime seats for the upcoming Saturday night game. He smiled as he thought about the enjoyment the kids would experience watching a professional basketball game and the pre-game autograph session. Danté especially would love it. He'd been talking about catching a game for months. He checked his watch. Danté was due for his math tutoring ten minutes ago. Normally, he wouldn't be concerned, but Monday Danté appeared distant, even turned down the ice cream Sam promised. If Sam wasn't preoccupied with his breakup with Kayla, he would have inquired more. Now as worry took over, he regretted allowing his personal life to interfere with his work.

As far as Kayla was concerned, he now had a peace about their situation, thanks to much prayer. She still refused to talk to him, but yesterday when he returned home, he found the tray with the clean dishes outside his door. The mere fact that Kayla ate the food and washed the dishes was a good sign that her anger was subsiding. If he could only be so sure about Danté.

He checked his watch again then picked up the phone to dial Danté's mother. After the sixth ring, he replaced the receiver on the base. Sam bowed his head and prayed for Danté's safety, but before the closing amen, his cell phone vibrated. The number on the caller ID was a welcomed reprieve from his worry.

"How is my favorite girl doing?" It was his mother.

"You better not let Kayla hear you say that. She might get jealous." Stella giggled into the phone. "Then again, she might not since the two of you are just friends."

"Okay, Mom, you got me. I do care about Kayla," Sam admitted without revealing exactly how much he cared.

"I knew it," Stella hollered into the phone. "I can't wait to meet my future daughter-in-law. I've been praying for the two of you to come together in God's time."

Sam shifted in his seat. Now might not be the best time to mention Kayla's religious views. "Hold on, Mom, it's not that simple."

"Do you love her?"

If he charged a fee every time someone had asked him that very question in the past three days, he'd have a small fortune. "Yes, Mother, but I suspect you've known that for quite a while."

"Of course, I'm your mother." Stella giggled once again. "I've just been waiting for you to realize it. Rachelle and I are coming to meet her Memorial Day weekend."

"Oh, really?" This was news to Sam.

"I guess I forgot to mention that little detail. The airlines had a sale." Stella laughed briefly before turning serious. "Son, I called because I wanted to check on you. Your health has been on my mind all day. Are you sick?"

"No, Mama, but thanks for checking."

A pregnant pause followed.

"Sam, be careful and give Kayla my love."

"I love you, Mama. See you in a couple of months."

Stella returned the sentiment and then hung up.

Before he could ponder his mother's warning, a hostile and unfamiliar voice yelled his name. Sam stood to see who the voice belonged to.

"Where is Sam? I want Sam."

Sam didn't recognize the dark-skinned man in the blue jeans and checkered flannel shirt with slurred speech and staggered walk.

Bobby Chen Li stepped from his office and into the hallway. "What's going on?"

"I want Sam," the stranger screamed again, this time louder.

Sam stepped into the hallway and stood face to face with the angry man. The alcohol stench instantly made Sam feel nauseated. With a hand signal he communicated to Bobby, who was standing behind the intruder, to secure the children and call the police. Bobby swiftly turned and ran.

"I am Samuel Jerrod. How can I help you?"

"You can't do nothing for me," the man slurred. "You've done enough already."

Something was familiar about the man, but Sam couldn't place him. "I'm sorry, but have we met before?"

"Don't play stupid with me. You know who I am." He swayed and blew his hot breath in Sam's face. "It's because of you my son doesn't respect me. He can't stand to be around me."

"Excuse me?"

"Because of you everything I try isn't good enough for him. All Danté talks about is Sam this and Sam that. That boy thinks you're some kind of saint. But you're not and here's what I think of you."

Sam didn't duck fast enough. Danté's father hawked and spat in his face. The film landed on his nose. Sam used his shirt sleeve to wipe the slimy substance from his face. Danté's father took advantage and sucker-punched Sam in the stomach.

"That's what you get for turning my son against me," he yelled as Sam bent over, gripping his mid-section. I may not be educated like you, but that doesn't give you the right to poison my son."

Filled with anger, Sam contemplated his next move. He could fight the intoxicated maniac or allow him to rant until the police arrived. Aaron Thomas was the same height as he, but a lot thinner. He had some nerve blaming him for his son not respecting him after the man beat the child and his mother, nearly killing them.

"That's enough," Bobby Chen Li yelled when Aaron punched Sam in the face.

Bobby was back and that meant the children were secure and the police were en route. Sam made up his mind to fight the guy. He positioned himself upright and prepared to land a left punch. Neither he nor Bobby saw the shiny six-inch blade until Aaron launched it into Sam's abdomen just above the waist.

From behind, Bobby knocked Aaron unconscious with a chair and then went to Sam's aide.

Sam now lay on the floor. He had pulled the knife out and covered the hole in his flesh with his hands. Blood gushed and seeped through his fingers and spilled onto the blue carpet.

Bobby grabbed the nearest phone and dialed 911 for the second time in five minutes. "Hold on, man," Bobby said when Sam's body began to shake. He removed his shirt and used it to cover the wound.

Sam lost control of his bodily fluids, as his body shook and his eyelids blinked rapidly. Cold darkness filled his body as warmth slowly seeped from his pores. Fear sucked the air from his lungs. "Mama," he managed between gasps. Gradually his vision darkened and the ringing in his ears grew louder. "Oh, God," rang from Sam's throat just before all went black.

～～～

The melody to Luther Vandross' "Dance With My Father" permeated through the store's overhead sound system and for once the song didn't bring tears to Kayla's eyes. What she felt now was closer to resentment toward her father for cheating her out of their first dance and numerous other special events. Kayla pushed thoughts of what could have been to the back of her mind and focused on the summer fashion display. Despising her father sapped too much of her energy. It was Wednesday, hump day as she called it, and she'd finally recovered from her emotionally draining weekend. Her appetite had returned with a vengeance, thanks to Sam's culinary skills. Since eating the breakfast he'd prepared the previous day, she'd practically been eating nonstop. With a full stomach, the mood swings subsided. Much to her dismay, she once again had Sam to thank for restoring her life back to normal.

She stood back and admired the display. Just months earlier she'd stocked the same rack with the latest fall and winter fashions. Although she doubted it, Kayla hoped love was like clothes: after a few months, they disappeared from the rack to make room for something new. If her wish came true, Samuel Jerrod would be out of her system by the fall, or at least by next summer. "Yeah, right," she grumbled. Chances of her ever completely getting over him were slim to none, but he would never be privileged to that information.

"Did you say something?" Ashley asked from her left side. She'd been avoiding Kayla as much as possible since she threatened to fire her three days ago.

"I was just thinking out loud." Kayla looked up to make eye contact, but Ashley looked away.

"I'm leaving in an hour for lunch. Is there anything you need me to do before I go, Ms. Perez?"

Kayla reached out and touched her arm. "Ashley, can we please talk?"

Ashley folded her arms. "You're the boss, you can say whatever you like and I'm required to listen."

"Ashley, I was wrong the other day. I was angry at Sam and took it out on you." Kayla squeezed her arm and smiled. "Come on, you know I wouldn't fire my right-hand girl."

Ashley smiled back. "Next time don't take three days to apologize."

"Trust me, I will never allow man drama to interfere with my professionalism again." They shared a light hug.

"Have you settled your differences with Sam?" Ashley inquired. "You guys make a cute couple."

Kayla held her hand up. "Sam and I are history and no, I do not want to talk about it."

"We'll save that conversation for after lunch," Ashley teased. "I don't care what you say, Sam is not history. You're in love with that man."

Kayla rolled her eyes at the runaway church girl. Ashley must have what Pastor Simmons called discernment. "How I feel or don't feel about Samuel Jerrod is irrelevant. I never want to see him again."

"Hmm." Ashley raised an eyebrow. "You used first and last name. Whatever he did was bad, but you still love him."

Kayla gave up. Once Ashley made up her mind about something it was useless trying to convince her otherwise. Besides, in this case her assessment was correct.

Kayla collected the debris from the floor. "Believe whatever you like," she said and then started for the dumpster.

"Kayla!"

Carlos' voice startled her and caught the attention of shoppers. She dropped the plastic and cardboard and turned to face her brother. The raw fear in his eyes and his red skin tone frightened her. The muscles in her chest constricted and breathing became labored.

"What's wrong with Mama?" she asked when he reached her, not caring that customers were watching and listening.

"Mama is fine." He paused. "It's Sam."

"What?" Kayla didn't understand why her brother would show up at her place of employment frantic over the likes of Samuel Jerrod. "What does Sam have to do with anything?"

"Mija, I'm sorry to have to tell you this, but Sam's been stabbed. He's undergoing emergency surgery right now at the county trauma center."

From behind her, Kayla heard Ashley gasp, but she wasn't moved. "You must be mistaken. I talked to him yesterday morning." She bent to pick up the bundle she'd dropped.

Carlos grabbed her by the shoulders. "It happened this afternoon at the Youth Center."

Kayla shook her head, although she knew Sam spent Wednesday afternoons at the center. The sound of Ashley's voice praying behind her caused her head to jerk back.

"It's true," Carlos continued. "I was having lunch with Jasmine—"

"Jasmine?" she cut him off. "Oh, yeah, I met her the other day at the church. Anyway, we were in the middle of lunch when someone from the church named Tyrell called her."

Kayla began to shake and gasp for air. "Some kid, Donnie or Dontel, his father came to the center and attacked Sam. It's pretty serious; he lost a lot of blood. Jasmine is making arrangements for his mother to fly in from Chicago."

Kayla saw Carlos' lips move, but she could not understand him. Her brother no longer made sense. True, Sam worked at the Youth Center and his best friend's name was Tyrell. And yes, Jasmine also worked in the church travel office, but Sam was not in some operating room clinging between life and death. Not her Sam.

"I have to call him," she said as she stood and reached for her cell phone.

Carlos grabbed her hands. "Mija, listen to me. Sam has been stabbed. He's in surgery at county."

Kayla's eyes slammed shut as the finality of Carlos' words penetrated her brain. Her head shook violently as visions of Sam, happy and healthy, flashed before her. Memories of his touch and his scent collided with the sound of his voice. Pounding that began in her chest quickly spread throughout her entire body. "Oh, God, please!" she wailed repeatedly.

Carlos lifted her into his arms before she fell to the floor. He started for her office, but Kayla redirected him. "Take me to him," she yelled. "I have to see him."

Carlos retraced his steps out the store.

"Don't worry about the store," Ashley called after her. "I'll call my mother and ask her to contact the intercessors at the church."

~~~

"Mija, are you sure about this?" Carlos asked after he placed the gear shift in park. Kayla insisted he make a stop before heading to the hospital.

Kayla fixed her eyes on the contemporary building structure and answered her brother. "If I don't do this now, I never will." She leaned her head against the window. "In some strange way, I think this happened to get me to this point."

Carlos rubbed her shoulder. "What about Sam?"

"I have to do this first, for me. Then I'll go to him."

Carlos didn't try to convince her otherwise. "I'll be waiting right here."

"Thank you," she said without taking her eyes away from the building. She opened the door and exited the vehicle. Once outside, she surveyed the parking lot. Cars were scattered around; therefore, she guessed the front doors would be unlocked. Slowly, but deliberately she walked to the entrance. The intimidation that massive structure once held over her had vanished. Relief washed over her when she turned the knob and the door opened. Tears instantly flowed down her cheeks and met at her chin the moment her feet touched the magenta carpet. By the time she made it to the doors of the main sanctuary sobs accompanied the tears.

Through blurred vision, she continued down the long aisle that led to the object that both beckoned her and haunted her dreams. With each step, her heart broke a little more until she was bent over, wailing from an internal ache. Her burdens were so heavy, by the time she reached the stage steps she fell to her knees. With determination she crawled across the stage to the foot of the wooden cross and for the first time cried out from the pit of her soul. "God, please help me!"

She hadn't read the manual on repentance. Not quite sure how to ask God to come into her life, Kayla allowed the words to flow unrehearsed and uncensored.

"God, please show me how to stop hating you and blaming you for every bad thing that has happened to me. Forgive me for all the bad things I said about you. I was angry. I really didn't mean it. Show me how to open up and allow you to love me. I really want you to love me, but I don't know how to let you in. I want to experience a relationship with you directly, but I don't know how. Everybody talks about how loving and caring you are. I want to experience that. Show me how to let go of my past hurts. I am so tired of hurting. I hurt so much. I am tired of hurting. Please take the pain away and love me and show me how to love you in return."

Kayla lowered her head in her hands and cried hot and heavy tears until she felt a soft touch on her shoulder. She looked up to find Pastor Simmons standing over her with tears streaming down his face.

Pastor Simmons fell to his knees beside Kayla and embraced her. Now that her spirit was broken her resistance was gone, she allowed the man she'd been fascinated by and yet distrusted for no apparent reason, to cuddle her in his arms like a baby. Her body heaved and shook as Pastor Simmons prayed fervently in her ear.

Tears of sorrow transcended into joyful drops as Kayla felt healing and forgiveness overwhelm her. Healing from the scars unjustly inflicted upon her and forgiveness for all those who had caused her to hurt. Her deceased father, the woman who sentenced her to a life of condemnation, the man who stole her innocence and the man she loved who lay in the balance between life and death.

"God, please help me to live on the inside and grant Sam a long happy life, even if it's without me."

Pastor Simmons continued to hold her and speak peace over her spirit. The more tremors racked her body, the harder he prayed.

"Mija?" Neither Pastor Simmons nor Kayla heard Carlos enter the empty sanctuary. "We should get to the hospital."

Kayla squeezed Pastor Simmons.

"I'll take care of her," the pastor answered, still holding her and looking over his shoulder.

Kayla broke down again.

Carlos looked up and stared at the cross long and hard before exiting.

Chapter 17

F ather, I thank you for sparing his life. Thank you
for extending Your loving grace and mercy to him
and for giving him another chance to serve You.
Father, please restore him back to complete health, even
better health than before. And God, show him how to
forgive the man who did this to him. I ask this in the
name of Your beloved son, Jesus. Amen."

Suspended between awareness and an anesthetic-
induced rest, Sam attempted to join in with the prayer
his mother prayed, but his brain wouldn't communicate
the desire to his mouth quick enough. Like the three
previous times he'd drifted into a semiconscious state,
pictures of Danté's father collided with images of his
mother kneeling beside her bed, praying. He shuddered as
chills caressed his body and then relaxed as warm hands
glided over his shoulders and arms. Before, he could open
his eyes and thank his mother for her comfort, darkness
claimed him once again, only to have the cycle repeat.

Several rotations later, a deep voice permeated from Danté's father's image, but the voice didn't match. Panic and fear filled Sam as his body began to vibrate. Fighting to wake up, his eyelids quivered.

"It's about time you woke up. You had me worried for a minute."

Slowly his eyes opened, but the bright light hanging over his bed caused him to shut them immediately.

"I know the drugs got you feeling good, but it's time to rejoin the real world."

Sam laid his head to the side and half-smiled, before attempting to open his eyes again. Although his vision was hazy, he recognized his best friend's worried expression. Tyrell looked tired and worn out in the black hooded sweatshirt. His eyes were red.

"Tee," he whispered.

"That's right, wake up. God is not ready for you yet."

Sam attempted a light chuckle, but when sharp pain radiated through his body, Sam flinched then attempted to sit up.

With care, Tyrell eased him back down. "Take it easy, man; you have a long way to go."

One sudden movement and all the subconscious visions made sense. The confrontation with Danté's drunken father replayed in his head up to the second Aaron Thomas stabbed him and he lay bleeding on the floor of the Youth Center. He remembered being transcended back in time to his childhood when his mother used to nurture his pain away. He wasn't sure if he called her name or not, but he felt the presence of God before succumbing to darkness.

He looked down at the bandage around his waist. "How bad is it?" he asked solemnly almost afraid to hear the answer.

Tyrell rested a hand on Sam's shoulder. "You have some tissue damage, but you are indeed a blessed man. If the blade had been just one fraction of an inch to the left, your spleen would have been filleted. You lost enough blood to require a transfusion, but God is good. In place of Bible study, the church held a special prayer session for you."

Sam's eyes glossed over and his heart swelled with gratefulness for a merciful God and a caring church family. "Prayer works, especially the prayers of a praying mother."

"Mama Stella began praying the second she heard my voice over the phone. She said the Lord had troubled her spirit."

"That's my mama." Sam briefly reflected on their conversation. Stella Jerrod was definitely in tune with her children. "When she gets back, I'll tell her she can stop praying. I'm fine." He paused. "Did she go back to my apartment to rest?"

Confusion veiled Tyrell's face. "What are you talking about?" He checked his watch. "Her plane doesn't land for another thirty minutes."

"It must be the drugs. I thought I heard her praying throughout the night." He attempted to raise his head to look out the window, but the room had none. "It is morning, right?"

"Yes, it is," Tyrell answered. "It's a quarter to eleven."

"And?" Sam knew his friend too well. Tyrell left something out and by the smile on his face, it was something good.

"You did hear a female praying from around midnight up until about an hour ago." He deliberately paused. "But it wasn't your mother. It was Kayla."

Excitement resulted in a fresh wave of pain when Sam attempted to bolt upright. Grunting and gritting his teeth, he fell back.

"Take it easy, man. Those bandages are there for a reason."

"Kayla? My Kayla?" he panted and clenched his fist. "Kayla Alicia Perez who lives in apartment two-twelve and loves to shop online, was here, praying?"

"Yes, she sure was," Tyrell answered with a grin. "Pastor Simmons dropped her off just before midnight."

"Pastor Simmons?" he interrupted, still panting.

"The hospital allows clergy to visit around the clock, but I don't think the sole reason he brought her was to help her to get past security. Anyway, Pastor stayed awhile and we prayed for you and then Kayla took over and prayed practically all night long for you. She rubbed your arms and shoulders with oil from the church."

Sam's breathing was almost back to normal. "Are you serious? I thought it was my mother's voice I heard."

"Yes, I think it's safe to say, Kayla's saved. And she prays beautifully, like a seasoned prayer warrior."

Tears formed and pooled at the corners before trickling down Sam's cheeks. He was speechless. Honestly, he hadn't anticipated her receiving salvation so soon. "Where is she?" he whispered, trying to downplay his need for her.

"She said she was going home to take a nap before her appointment with Pastor Simmons."

"Oh." Sam was both happy and saddened by Kayla spending time with his spiritual leader. Pastor Simmons was a psychologist by profession and could help Kayla in ways he could not. But he still desired to see her, to witness the miracle. "Is she coming back?"

"I don't know," Tyrell answered honestly. "She didn't say."

Once again Sam disguised his disappointment with a slight chuckle, but scolded himself for being selfish. Kayla had spent the entire night with him and in his opinion that was more than he deserved. He closed his eyes and envisioned her at the foot of his bed, praying. Suddenly, his eyes bulged.

"What about Danté?" He panted, not from pain, but from fear for the child's safety.

"Calm down." Tyrell tapped his shoulder. "Danté is safe, now."

"Now?"

"Yeah, now." Tyrell sat in the chair next to the bed. "Bobby came by while you were in recovery. After the ambulance brought you here, he and the police went to Danté's house to check on him. Apparently, Danté's father was angry because his son didn't want to hang out with him. Danté wanted to come to the Youth Center for his session with you. When Danté's mother refused to make the boy go along, his father became angry. The old monster returned, and he beat her unconscious, then left. Bobby found Danté hiding behind the washing machine. Poor kid. His mother is in the hospital, his no-good father is in jail, and he's in the custody of Child Protective Services."

"Oh no," Sam moaned. "I have to go get him."

Tyrell smirked. "And just how do you plan to do that? You can't get out of this bed."

Sam's hands roamed the bedside table. "Where's the phone? I have to call somebody."

"Don't worry, he's safe. CPS granted Bobby temporary custody until his mother recovers. The good news is his mother regained consciousness and pressed charges this time."

Sam half-smiled. "Great. Physically, Danté is safe, but I'll have to deprogram all of Bobby's doctrinal beliefs."

Tyrell hunched his shoulders. "Maybe not. Yesterday, he prayed with us and he wasn't chanting. As a matter of fact, he yelled 'Jesus'."

They shared a laugh and then quieted down. For a prolonged period of time the only sound in the room was the rhythmic beep of the machine measuring his heart rate and oxygen level.

"God sure works in mysterious ways." Tyrell broke the silence.

Sam swallowed the emotions hovering in his throat. "When I felt that knife tear my body, I thought I was about to die. My world was coming to an end. But God said, 'Not so'." He began to pray out loud before sleep claimed him once again.

Chapter 18

Kayla heard the commotion in the hallway and quickly ran to her front door. With caution, she cracked the door open to keep from being detected and peeked through the small opening. "Thank you, Father," she whispered from behind the door.

Gratitude and love overwhelmed her as she watched Sam, with the assistance of Tyrell, enter his apartment for the first time since the stabbing seven days ago. His muscular physique looked wonderful now that he was standing and not laying in a hospital bed hooked up to machines. The two women, following behind with grocery bags, she guessed were Sam's mother and sister. Both were dressed in outfits she'd selected for Christmas. Kayla listened to the tall woman with slightly salted hair reprimand Sam for trying to walk too fast and wished she was the one taking care of him. She owed him that for all he'd done for her, but Kayla didn't know how to be there for him.

She hadn't spoken to Sam, but she did check in with Tyrell daily for updates. During her counseling sessions with Pastor Simmons, he assured her of Sam's well-being. Both Pastor Simmons and Tyrell encouraged her to visit Sam in the hospital, but she couldn't bring herself to do so. She prayed for him every morning and night and not just for his physical heath. Kayla entreated God for his spiritual strength and for him to fulfill his call to the ministry. What she desired more than anything was for Sam to be happy. Where did she fit in the equation, she didn't know, but Sam would always hold a special place in her heart.

"I want you to go straight to bed," Kayla heard his mother order once Tyrell got the door open.

"But Mama," Sam whined.

"But nothing." His mother ignored his pouting.

"You heard Mama," his sister added.

Sam turned around and Kayla closed the door.

She leaned against the door a long time and wished the slab of wood was Sam's chest. She closed her eyes and drifted back to that day he rescued her at the ice-skating rink. Sam always knew exactly how to comfort her. Now she wished she hadn't broken the music box. Reluctantly, she released the door knob and walked into her bedroom.

It amazed her how one simple addition made her entire room feel different. The framed photo of "Footprints in the Sand" that now hung over her bed changed the atmosphere. Her bedroom had become a place of serenity and rest. The picture was a gift from Pastor Simmons to celebrate her new life in Christ. "God never leaves us and He never stops loving us," he told her that day at the foot of the cross. For the first time in her life Kayla believed those words and received comfort.

After reading the poem, she sat down on her bed and picked up her new student study Bible, another gift from Pastor Simmons. He had given her scriptures to read to help teach her about Christ. Thus far, in seven days she'd learned so much, joy overflowed from her. At work she shared her new life with Ashley and in the evenings, she talked with her mother. "I told you, you are a Christian," Rozelle said proudly. Kayla hadn't had the chance to share with Carlos. He was too busy spending time with Jasmine. Kayla made a mental note to find out what that was all about.

Her reading assignment for the day was Psalm 30. Like the psalmist, she cried out to God and He healed her. He brought her soul up from the grave and for the first time in her life, she felt like she was truly alive. "God, I thank you," she whispered and then continued reading.

Early the next morning Kayla finished packing the basket. She'd purchased a big basket from the dollar store and stuffed it with all of Sam's favorite snacks. She included fresh fruit and a new pair of pajamas with matching house slippers. At the last minute she stopped at the Bible bookstore for DVDs from his favorite television evangelist and a journal with his name engraved on it.

She stepped back from the table and admired her creation. She conceded she'd gone overboard, but Sam was worth it. For now, he still held her heart. Kayla braced herself to lift the heavy basket. She opened her front door then tiptoed across the hall to his apartment. It was 8:00 a.m. and she figured someone would be up, but she wasn't ready to see him. Kayla eased the basket down in front of his door. She didn't have a card, but figured once Sam saw the red pajamas, he'd know where the basket came from. Kayla pressed the doorbell then turned to sprint back to her apartment. Unfortunately for her, she ran right into Sam's mother.

"It's nice to finally meet you, Kayla," Stella said once she steadied herself.

Kayla stood there with her mouth hanging open and eyes bulging.

"Don't look so shocked," Stella continued. "Sam has told me all about you. I must admit, I was surprised you didn't stop by the hospital." She looked down at the monstrous basket. "That's some package. I'd certainly give that gift to a friend." Stella smiled mischievously.

"Well, I," Kayla fumbled over her words. "I was just—I was on my way to work."

Stella laughed out loud. "Do I make you nervous?"

Kayla swallowed hard. The woman before her did in fact make her nervous. Up close the resemblance to Sam was striking. He was the spitting image of his mother minus the hair and earrings. "Hello, Ms. Jerrod. I've heard so much about you." Kayla smiled uneasily.

"Don't be so formal, we're practically family, Stella is fine. Besides, I feel like I know you already. Sam described you perfectly." She removed a key from her pocket. "Good thing I went for a walk this morning at the marina, or we would have never met. Come on inside so we can chat."

"I have to get to work," Kayla said, looking back at her apartment.

"That's right," Stella said and folded her arms then leaned against the wall. "You work at a clothing store. You have very good taste. I get compliments every time I wear the clothes Sam sent me."

Kayla took a step backward. "Thank you, Ms. Stella. Maybe we'll have a chance to talk later." She turned to leave, but before she could take a step, Stella's next question made her stop mid-stride.

"Kayla, do you love my son?" The direct question caught Kayla off guard. She debated on how to answer. Should she be evasive or just plainly refuse to answer? She decided to tell the truth. She turned back around and faced her. "Yes, I do," she admitted. "But we're just friends, at least we were." Kayla lowered her head and began counting the specks in the carpet.

Stella stepped to her and lifted her chin and forced Kayla to make eye contact. "Take the basket inside. I know he wants to see you."

"I want to see him too," she confessed. "But I'm not ready. I have to work on myself first."

Stella nodded her understanding and placed her hand on Kayla's shoulder. "Alright, I'll be praying for you."

"Thank you," she whispered and covered Stella's hand.

"Mom, did you forget your key?" Sam called from inside the apartment.

The door knob turned.

"I have to go." Kayla turned and ran. Before she made it inside the confines of her unit, she heard Stella say, "I just met my daughter-in-law."

Kayla slammed the door and bolted the lock.

~~~

Sam stepped aside to let his mother pass. "What did you say?"

"Rachelle, come help me lift this basket," Stella called down the hall. She turned back to Sam. "How are you feeling this morning? Give me a few minutes and I'll make you some breakfast."

Sam leaned against the door for support. "I'm fine. Rachelle cooked."

His sister brushed past. "Mama, where did you find all this stuff?"

Stella grinned at Sam. "I didn't find anything. I caught Sam's future wife playing doorbell ditch this morning."

Rachelle stepped into the hallway. "I can't wait to meet her. Where is she?"

Sam looked down at the basket. A smile slowly crept across his face. "Kayla was here?"

"I thought that would bring a smile to your face. Now go sit down before you hurt yourself."

Sam eased his body onto the couch. Rachelle and Stella set the gift basket beside him. Temporarily he forgot about the pain in his abdomen and savored Kayla's thoughtfulness. He was beginning to think she no longer cared. She hadn't returned to the hospital and whenever he inquired of her Tyrell and Pastor Simmons both encouraged him to continue to pray for her, which he did daily.

He held the pajamas to his chest and wished the red fabric was Kayla. How he longed for just one drama queen moment. He traced the gold lettering embossed on the journal. "She has exquisite taste." The words weren't meant to be heard, but Stella's hearing was keen.

"She sure does. And she's beautiful," Stella commented.

"I wish I could have met her." Rachelle pouted. "What's she like?"

Without hesitation, Sam described Kayla from head to toe. He even mentioned her shopping habits and favorite foods. When he finished, Sam leaned back on the couch, with the pajamas still in his hand.

"Rachelle, go and change your brother's bed linen. I need to talk to him."

"Okay, but let me know if Kayla comes back."

Stella waited until she heard Sam's bedroom door close. "Son," she said as she removed the pajamas and placed them back inside the basket. "What's the real story behind Kayla? Why is she afraid to see you?"

He deeply exhaled. "Our relationship is complicated."

Stella looked around the room. "Does it look like I'm going anywhere?"

Sam chuckled at his mother's directness. "Mama, I ended our relationship once I realized I was in love with her?"

Stella looked perplexed. "Why?"

"Up until a few days ago, Kayla didn't believe in God."

Stella raised an eyebrow. "Oh really?"

"Many bad things have happened to her that caused her to be angry with God. She wouldn't even step foot inside of a church."

"But now all that's changed. I know I saw God in her. I also saw fear," Stella observed. "What I don't understand is why the two of you can't have a relationship now that she's saved?"

Sam rubbed his forehead. "I haven't seen Kayla and she won't talk to me. I believe she still cares, but she's avoiding me. Leaving this basket at the door is proof. She doesn't want to see me."

Stella patted his leg. "Don't worry, son. It will work out in God's time. I know what I saw in her eyes this morning."

"How can you be so sure?"

"Her mouth confirmed what her eyes told me."

Sam pressed her. "Exactly what did she say?"

Stella shook her head. "I'm not going to tell you. You're a man of God. Why don't you pray and ask Him about it?" Stella left him alone on the couch.

Chapter 19

S am sat on the couch with the remote control in his hand. He completed the third cycle of channel surfing without any luck of finding anything of value to watch. The thought occurred to him to use his downtime to write the major networks and request better quality programming. A person could tolerate only so many crime scene investigation and Court TV shows before going insane. He reached his limit five days after returning home. Now, on the tenth day, he settled for old sitcoms and game shows.

He walked over to his entertainment center and selected one of the DVDs Kayla purchased. In the midst of deciding between the two, which he'd seen at least three times already, the doorbell sounded. As quickly as his impaired body would allow, Sam walked to the door. He hoped it was Kayla playing another game of doorbell ditch. If it were, they'd finally have a chance to talk since his mother and sister were out on a trip to catch a sale on toilet paper and toothpaste at a national discount store. For ten days he'd been trying to catch her leaving or entering her apartment and praying for her to stop by, but nothing. He called and left three messages on both her home and cell phones with no response, yet his hopes were high. He flung the door open with expectation and lowered his eyes to the floor in anticipation of another surprise package. The brown package was three-and-a-half-feet tall.

"Hey, Danté," Sam exclaimed. His injury prevented him from bending over to hug his little friend. Instead, Sam wrapped his arm around Danté's shoulders and pulled him close to his side. "How have you been?"

Danté's little arms squeezed Sam's waist. He then looked up at Sam. "Okay. I just came to say good-bye."

"Good-bye?" Confused, Sam looked up at Bobby and Danté's mother. Both looked sad, but Sherri Thomas' face was also discolored and a bandage covered her left eye.

"Come in." Sam stepped aside to allow his guests to enter.

Danté remained by his side while his mother slowly maneuvered into the chair adjacent to the couch.

Bobby remained standing. "You're getting around better than the last time I saw you." Bobby had visited Sam three times since his discharge from the hospital. On each occasion they shared a word of prayer and Sam heard Bobby call on Jesus with his own ears. "The process is moving right along."

Danté's fingers felt the bandages. "What happened to you?" he asked Sam.

Sam looked over at Bobby whose facial expression confirmed that he'd honored Sam's wishes for Danté not to know that his father tried to kill him. Bobby and Sam agreed the information would only traumatize the child more.

"Bobby said you were in the hospital. Are you better now?"

Sam gazed into the child's expectant eyes. "Yes, I'm better now. I don't want to talk about me. I want to know why you came all the way over here to tell me good-bye."

Danté looked over at his mother.

"It's okay for you to tell him," Sherri said and lowered her head.

"We're moving to India tonight," Danté announced.

"India?" Sam exclaimed. "Wow, that's far."

"Baby, it's Indiana not India," Sherri corrected her son.

Sam directed his question to both Sherri and Bobby. "Is that a good idea?" Danté's father was in jail with a charge of attempted murder and a list long enough to lock him up for a long time, but Sam was still concerned for Danté.

"We have family there. My relatives have tried for years to talk me into moving back, but I refused. This last episode was enough to finally convince me."

Sam nodded his understanding then refocused on Danté.

"You're going to like Indiana. I used to live down the street in Chicago. My mother and my brother and sisters still live there. When I come home to visit them, I'll come see you too.

Danté liked that idea. "So we can still be friends?" he inquired.

Sam squeezed him. "We will always be friends. You can even have my phone number."

"I already gave it to him," Bobby said from behind. "He has mine as well. I told him that you and I can help him with his spelling and reading via cell phone or webcam."

"That's right," Sam confirmed.

Danté twisted his face. "But what if I don't need help? Can I still call you?"

The pounding in Sam's chest made it difficult for him to imagine his life without Danté. Honestly, he didn't want the boy to leave. Being with Danté sufficed the yearning in him for children of his own. He looked into the child's expectant eyes. "You can call me anytime you want and for any reason. I'll be part of your life for as long as you want."

Danté giggled and then laid his head against Sam.

Bobby walked over and took Danté by the hand. "Hey, man, let's find something to eat. Your mom and Sam need to talk."

With curiosity Sam watched them trot off to the kitchen. He then turned to Sherri for an explanation. "What's going on?"

"Sam, I know you probably think I'm a bad parent for allowing Danté's father back into our life," she began.

He interrupted. "I'm not your judge."

"I know, but I also know you weren't pleased with my actions."

Sam remained quiet.

"I'm sorry for what happened to you. I never meant for you to be hurt." She paused. "I only allowed Aaron back, for Danté's sake."

Sam twisted his face. "Danté's sake?"

Sherri leaned forward. "Let me explain. I'm sick, dying actually."

"What?" Sam gasped.

"I have Lupus and it's aggressively attacking my body. Outside of a miracle, doctors have given me no more than three years to live."

"Oh, God," he whispered.

"I think I have less time than that. My body is tired." She paused to wipe her face with the back of her hand. "Anyway, I was hoping Aaron had changed so I wouldn't have to worry about Danté. That's why I gave him another chance. I wanted Danté to have a good relationship with his father before I left. I have accepted that's not going to happen and have made other arrangements for my son's care."

"Is that why you're moving back to Indiana? So your family can care for him?"

Sherri shook her head. "I'm moving back home so my family can care for me during my last days. Danté doesn't know about the Lupus. I'll tell him once we're settled. After I'm gone," she paused, "Danté will return to California—to you."

Sam leaned against the back of the couch for support. "I don't understand," he said, shaking his head.

"My family is a wonderful group of people, but Danté doesn't really know them. My parents are older and already care for my sister's two children. Adding one more would be too much for them. I've already talked to them and on yesterday I met with an attorney and had the appropriate documents drawn up. At my demise, you will have complete custody of Danté until he's of age."

Sam's breath caught in his throat and what energy he had evaporated. He staggered around the couch and sank onto its cushions.

"I know this is a surprise, but I also know it's the right decision. I prayed about it and God showed me the love you have for my son. I hear in his voice, almost daily, how much Danté adores you. The two of you will be good together." Sherri paused to blow her nose. Sam remained speechless. "I have two life insurance policies and a trust set up to financially provide for Danté. My attorney will send you all the information in the mail." She reached into her purse and pulled out a business card. "You can contact him at this number." Mechanically, Sam took the card and placed it on the coffee table. He didn't say anything.

"Sam, I want to thank you for reaching out to my boy. I believe this last ordeal would have destroyed him if you had not been in his life. Bobby told me, every day he asked about you and the only way he could get him to calm down was to promise to bring him to see you."

Thoughts bombarded Sam's mind at a rapid pace. So much made sense to him now. His paternal awareness didn't come alive until he met Danté. Whenever he had thoughts of the future, Danté was always in the picture. Now he knew why.

"Sherri, I don't know what to say. I'm honored and flattered. And yes, I do love Danté. I promise I will raise him with the same love I'll give my future biological children."

Relief washed Sherri's face. "Thank you. I can leave California and this earth in peace."

Sam made eye contact with Bobby and his expression conveyed all the words he could not say in Danté's presence.

Sherri stood. "We should get going. We have a few more stops to make before going to the train station."

Slowly Sam lifted his body from the couch. "Before you leave, can we pray?"

The three adults held hands in a circle and prayed with Danté leaning his head against Sam's tall frame.

"Can you tell Ms. Kayla I said good-bye and that I miss her?" Danté said at the end of the prayer.

Chapter 20

With every step forward Kayla's heart rate accelerated, but she didn't dare stop. The excitement of her new life overrode the fear of the unknown. She was certain of one thing, the life before her was better than the one she was leaving behind. She looked down the row at her support system. She appreciated her family's encouragement, but Ashley's smile was the reinforcement she needed to continue on her journey to the front. The mere fact that Ashley stepped inside of a church for the first time in years, was proof that God had a purpose for her life. Kayla blocked out every sound, except Pastor Simmons' voice.

Sam stood on the platform with his head bowed in prayer. Standing before God's people, inviting them to accept Jesus Christ as savior and to become part of God's kingdom was something he never thought he would do again as he lay bleeding on the floor a month ago. God had spared his life, and in the process, blessed him with a son. For that he was so grateful. Every day he prayed for Sherri's health and for God to prepare him for fatherhood. That had become his top priority.

Tyrell nudged him. "Look who's joining the church."

Sam opened his eyes and looked in Pastor Simmons' direction. "Oh, my God!" he gasped and then his eyes misted. The most beautiful woman on earth held his pastor's hand as tears streamed down her cheeks.

He hadn't seen Kayla since the night of the breakup. They hadn't talked in a month, but his heart hadn't released her. She was more beautiful than he remembered and he loved her more. He swallowed back the lump in his throat and whispered a prayer. "Father, thank you for bringing Kayla into the fold. Thank you for healing her broken heart." With pride he listened to Kayla and countless others confess salvation in Jesus Christ and then receive the right hand of fellowship at Grace Temple.

Following the custom at Grace Temple, Sam hurried to the fellowship hall after service for the New Members/ Visitors Reception. His breathing increased rapidly as he searched frantically for Kayla. He saw her parents and Carlos talking with Jasmine, but not Kayla. After casing the room for the third time without any success, he left defeated. Reality set in once again. Kayla didn't want to see him.

"Man, don't look so down," Tyrell said when he passed him in the vestibule on the way to his office. Sam waved him off and continued walking.

Somberly, Sam unlocked his office and removed his jacket and clergy collar. A white letter-sized paper on the floor caught his attention and he bent to pick it up. Someone slipped an auxiliary report underneath his door and figured he might as well enter the data now.

"Hello, Sam." With the force of a hammer, Kayla's voice stopped him dead in his trek to his seat behind his desk. He took a deep breath and then slowly turned to face her. Unlike the last time she spoke to him, anger and contempt were missing. In its place the softness his soul longed for.

"Hey, Kayla," he managed after he made his way around his desk to his chair and sat down.

"I bet you never thought you'd see me join church?"

His hands fiddled with the paper in his hands. "Of course, I did. I believe in the power of prayer."

Kayla stepped completely inside the office and sat down. "So do I—now." She smiled and he smiled back.

"I'm surprised you're here in my office. I was under the impression that you didn't want to see me."

Her smile suddenly disappeared, replaced by sincere concern. "Sam, I always wanted to see you, even when I was angry. When you got hurt that day, my life changed dramatically. It's been a rollercoaster ride ever since."

Sam absentmindedly folded the paper in half. "So I've vaguely heard from Pastor Simmons. I would have loved to have experienced the transition with you." At that moment Sam realized he was jealous of the role his pastor held in Kayla's life. Inwardly, he repented.

"I know you would have." She paused. "I hope you understand, but I had to do this on my own. I couldn't allow my feelings for you to be my motivation.

I had to seek God because I needed him, not because I wanted you."

Sam's nod indicated that he understood.

"When you got stabbed, I realized that harboring anger against God wasn't the solution to my pain. You were right, I needed counseling. Pastor Simmons has helped me release all that anger and bitterness from my father and Candace's death. As far as the rape, I'm learning how to forgive my attacker. And you, I can never hate you. In fact, you saved my life."

Sam stopped quarter folding the paper and raised an eyebrow. "I don't understand."

Kayla entwined her fingers together. "If you hadn't tricked me into going to that play on Christmas Eve, I would still be running. Truth be told, God began drawing me to Him that night."

"Glad I could be of help." Sam chuckled. An uneasy silence filled the room. "Thanks for the basket. As always, your taste is exquisite."

Kayla blushed and the folded paper fell from his hands. "I got your messages, but I wasn't ready to see you. I hope you understand?"

"I do now," he admitted. Pressing Kayla would have been a mistake. But what about now, he was afraid to ask, but decided to take a chance. "So, what's on your agenda now that you've joined church?"

"Well," she began by rubbing her hands together. "I have both short- and long-term goals. For the short term I'm going to continue my counseling sessions with Pastor Simmons. At the same time, I plan to attend the

New Converts class to learn more about the Lord and how to live this new life. I spent so long hating God that I want to make sure I love Him even harder."

Her sincerity touched his heart. "That's beautiful. What about the long term?"

Kayla bit her lower lip then stood to her feet and pointed a finger at him. "See that's where you come in."

Sam chuckled. Her body language was classic Drama Queen Kayla and he loved it. She was about to drop a bombshell. "I'm listening."

"See, I was thinking for the long term," she continued to point and walked around his desk, "you and I can resume dating and I don't mean that phony friendship thing either. I mean the kind of dating between a man and a woman who are destined to be together."

Sam's jaw fell.

"You can teach me how to bargain shop and I will teach you how to coordinate your clothing. Then, at God's appointed time, I will let you propose to me and I will accept your hand in marriage. I will limit my online shopping to once a month. And I will only require you to make me cinnamon French toast once a week. When you and I open a church, I'll sit on the front row with our children." Kayla placed her hands on her hips. "So, are you in or do I have to pray you into submission?"

Thunderous laughter poured from Sam. He couldn't believe it. His drama queen was back and already toiling with his emotions. In less than an hour Kayla had managed to drag him through elation, down to defeat, and now, up to sheer joy. Oh how he missed this woman.

"Well?" She patted her feet against the floor. "I'm waiting."

"Kayla, sweetheart, there's something I have to tell you?" He didn't miss the fear she tried to mask by blinking rapidly. "My life has changed dramatically as well. I'm going to be a father."

"Oh." Her shoulders slumped, all the bravado quickly vanished. "I see. I have to go." She turned to run from the office, but Sam caught her by the arms from behind.

"It's not what you think," he said as he held her stationary. "Let me explain, please."

She nodded. "I'm listening."

Without releasing his hold, Sam explained everything about Sherri's illness and her wishes.

"That poor baby," she said when he finished. "We should spend time with him in the meantime and be there with him when his mother passes. It'll make the transition easier." She paused. "I guess this means we'll have to move out of the complex. Kids should have a yard to play in." She stopped talking and turned to face him. "I would love to share my life with Danté. Now do we have a deal?"

Sam looked down into her eyes and decided to see just how much bargaining power he held. "Before I agree to your demands, can I have a kiss?"

Kayla held her ground. "Only my future husband will kiss these lips."

Sam wrapped his arms around her waist and closed the distance between them. "You always get your way with me, don't you?"

"It's only fair since you captured my heart."

She placed her arms around his neck. "I love you, Samuel Jerrod."

"I love you more." The words escaped inches before their lips met.

In the euphoria of the kiss, neither of them heard Stella enter the office. "Looks like things are finally in order. I can go home now."

Sam waved his mother away and continued the love dance with Kayla's lips.

Chapter 21

A second after she stepped inside her mother's dark house a loud blast sent Kayla tumbling to the floor.

"Surprise," everyone screamed. When the lights flickered on, the culprit was easy to spot. If she weren't so excited about celebrating her birthday, she would have punched Carlos in the face for blowing the horn directly in her ear.

Sam appeared from the crowd and pushed Carlos out of the way. "Sweetheart, are you okay?"

She glared at Carlos. "I will be." Kayla reached for Sam's outstretched arms and he easily lifted her to her feet.

They stood holding hands with their foreheads touching. "Happy birthday, beautiful," he said.

"Thank you, gorgeous." She giggled.

"I know he's not the only person you see?" Rozelle huffed from behind her.

Reluctantly, Kayla disengaged from Sam and faced not only her mother, but the small expectant crowd behind her. Everyone, who'd played a role in her transformation, was present. Pastor Simmons and his wife along with Tyrell and Jasmine joined in with Sam and her family in a chorus of Stevie Wonder's version of "Happy Birthday," led by Ashley and Bobby. That was a sight to behold, the runaway church girl and the master of all religions, doing an updated version of the "bump." "Lord, help them," she managed as she watched the playful exchange. She then hugged and greeted all of her surprise guests, except for her brother, who opted to lift her off the floor and spin her around.

"Happy birthday, mija." Carlos spun her around until she became dizzy then deliberately let her down off balanced. That was his tradition. Thankfully, Sam was there to steady her.

"Thank you all so much. I had no idea y'all were planning me a surprise birthday party," Kayla said as she leaned onto Sam for support.

"We didn't," her mother clarified. "This was all Sam's doing."

With adoration in her eyes, Kayla turned to Sam. "You are so good to me."

"You deserved it, sweetheart. You've had a hard year."

"True," Kayla pondered. "But it's also been the best year of my life, thanks to you." From behind, she heard Carlos gag. "Don't hate me because I'm in love," she said over her shoulder. "I give you two months before Jasmine has a noose around your heart."

The room erupted in laughter as everyone watched Jasmine, embarrassed, run into the kitchen.

"Jasmine and I are just friends," Carlos barked.

"What's new? So were your sister and Sam," Tyrell reminded him. "That seems to be how this family operates."

"That's right." Rozelle smirked. "Travis and I were friends for about ten years."

Pastor Simmons walked up beside Carlos and patted his shoulder. "I'll see you in Bible study."

Carlos mumbled something under his breath and then stomped into the kitchen to find Jasmine amid laughter.

"It's time to eat," Rozelle announced. "Then we can get to the festivities."

Kayla curiously eyed Sam and wondered what festivities he had in mind. Whatever they were, Kayla would enjoy them in the same manner she relished every day of their official courtship. For the first time in her memory, Kayla was happy with God, life and herself. Now that she was healed of her wounds, she appreciated and freely received the love around her. And the more she received the more she gave.

Sam gave her his best false innocent look and then ushered her into the dining room. Kayla said grace and afterward Sam served her. During dinner, Kayla noticed Rozelle filled her plate less than normal, but didn't bother to ask why. In the midst of savoring a crab stuffed mushroom Sam's cell phone sounded. Kayla recognized his mother's ring tone.

"Hold on a minute," he said and then handed the phone to Kayla.

"Happy birthday, Ms. Kayla," she heard on the other end. It was Danté.

Kayla's heart fluttered and she dropped her fork. The consideration Danté gave her was remarkable. She couldn't wait for him to become her son.

Sam leaned back in his chair and listened to the tender one-sided exchange. Gently, he laid his fork down on top of his napkin and then nodded at Rozelle.

"Come on, it's time to go back into the living room and get this party started." Rozelle and Travis stood. "You can bring your plates if you want to," Rozelle added.

Kayla, with the phone still attached to her ear, followed behind everyone. Sam was behind her. Once inside the living room, she stopped speaking into the phone and waved along with everyone else at the computer screen. Thanks to technology, Stella and Sam's siblings along with Sherri and Danté waved back at her and wished her a happy birthday with a paper sign.

"This is so sweet." She happily waved and then blew kisses. She was so caught up with the webcam, she didn't notice that Sam had knelt on one knee beside her. It wasn't until she heard Stella speak, "Look down," in the monitor did she look down.

"Oh, Sam," she whispered when he collected her left hand in his. "On my birthday?"

"Shush." Rozelle quieted the room.

"When I prayed this time last year," Sam began, "I asked God to reveal the wife He had designed for me.

Not once did I think she would come in the form of a cinnamon-French-toast-eating, online-shopping-addicted drama queen." He paused until the laughter in the room subsided. "But you're it. Kayla, you're everything I want in a wife and friend. The first time I saw you in the grocery store, from afar I knew in my heart you were a special person." Gently, he kissed her hand. "This past year, I have watched you transform from a wounded, scared and angry person into a strong, brave and happy beautiful loving young woman. You have so much love inside of you and I want to spend the rest of my life receiving that love." He reached inside his front shirt pocket and pulled out the ring.

Kayla's eyes bulged.

"Kayla Alicia Perez, will you do me the honor of allowing me to be your husband? I promise the only person I'll ever love more than you is God."

Kayla threw her head back and opened her mouth to respond, but before she could get the word out, Carlos yelled, "No!"

"No?" everyone questioned in unison.

"Excuse me, but I don't think he was talking to you," Kayla snapped at her brother. He'd just ruined the moment she'd been waiting in high anticipation for and she didn't like that.

"Well, as your older brother I'm answering for you. You cannot marry him." Carlos' nostrils flared and his caramel skin turned a shade darker.

Sam dropped his head and released Kayla's hand.

"Carlos Esteban Perez, stay out of their business," Rozelle yelled after slapping him on the back of the head.

"No, Ma, this is where I draw the line. Kayla cannot and will not marry that man." He pointed down at Sam.

Kayla's hands pushed against his chest. "I am a grown woman, you can't tell me what to do."

Carlos stood his ground. "In this case, I can. I will not allow this wedding to take place." Pastor Simmons intervened. "Carlos, what do you have against Sam? He's a good God fearing man."

"I don't care how good he is. He can't marry my sister." Carlos folded his arms with finality.

"Why, Carlos? I love him; why don't you want me to be happy?" Kayla broke down sobbing.

Sam stood and held her in his arms and looked back at the monitor. The faces staring back were confused.

"Why, Carlos?" Kayla asked again.

"Yeah, why can't she marry him?" Rozelle asked then the question echoed around the room. Every eye zeroed in on Carlos.

Carlos folded his arms across his chest and looked Sam dead in the eye. "You can't marry my sister because you didn't ask me first."

Rozelle along with everyone else threw their hands up in the air. "Boy, are you crazy? He asked me, that's enough. I'm her mother."

"No, Ma, that is not sufficient. As her older brother, in the absence of our father, I should have been consulted first."

Jasmine stood next to him, laughing at his bruised ego. He glared at her, but it was useless. The entire room enjoyed a laugh at his expense. Kayla even stopped crying and joined in.

Sam composed himself and extended his hand to Carlos. "Man, I am sorry. I didn't mean to overlook you." Sam paused to keep more laughter from erupting. "I love your sister and I want to spend the rest of my life with her. Can I please have her hand in marriage?"

Carlos' gaze bounced from Sam to Kayla. Both smiled and the others snickered around him. Determined to have his way, Carlos held his chin up and answered, "I'll think about it."

Both his mother and Jasmine reached up and hit him on the back of the head.

"Okay, okay," he cried out when Kayla pinched his arm. He rubbed the spot and then finally accepted Sam's outstretched hand. Surprisingly to everyone, after all the dissention, Carlos embraced Sam tightly.

Kayla interrupted the bonding. After all, it was her birthday. "Can I have my ring now?"

"Say the magic word and it's yours," Sam teased.

Once again, Kayla revved her head back and hollered, "Yes."

Finally, amid cheers and applause, Sam placed the ring on her shaky finger, but before he could kiss her, Kayla stepped aside and displayed her hand into the webcam where a sign reading, "Welcome to the family," hung upside down in Danté's hands.

Kayla's smile eased some when she noticed the strain on Sherri's face.

"Thank you," Sherri mouthed.

From behind, Sam's arms encircled her waist and while she continued to wave at his family he whispered in her ear, "You're going to make a great mother."

She leaned her head against him and braced herself for the adventure.

Group Discussion Questions

1. Considering the tragedies she endured, do you feel Kayla's resentment toward God was justified?

2. Sam was a leader in the church with ambition of pastoring. Do you feel it was wise for him to become involved with Kayla knowing his was attracted to her? Should believers date unbelievers?

3. Kayla's mother assumed Kayla believed in God because she sent Kayla to church as a child and came from a family of believers. Do you think this is a common misconception many parents make? How important is it for parents to have a direct conversation with their children about salvation?

4. Kayla felt God hated her because of all the bad things that had happened to her, although she was a good person. Is her rationale common amongst non-believers? Have you ever felt this way?

5. Do you agree with Sam's decision to end the relationship once he realized he was in love with Kayla? Why, or why not?

6. Sam had an accountability partner to help keep him focused on his purpose. In your opinion, do believers, especially leaders, have a hard time being accountable?

7. Why do you think Pastor Simmons led Kayla to salvation and healing, and not Sam?
8. What was your favorite scene in the story?
9. What lesson(s) do you learn from Kayla's Redemption that can be applied to your life?
10. Which characters would you like to read more about?

More titles by Wanda B. Campbell:

First Sunday in October – Simone Family Series Book 1

Games - Simone Family Series Book 2

Liberation - Simone Family Series Book 3

Unresolved Issues - Simone Family Series Book 4

Illusions

Right Package, Wrong Baggage

Silver Lining

Doin' Me

Back to Me

Under the Influence

Coming Soon:

Growing Pains – Journey Series Book 2

CPSIA information can be obtained
at www.ICGtesting.com
Printed in the USA
BVHW071447201221
624506BV00001B/214